# The Leftover

## A Relook on the Leftover Buddhist in the Indian Subcontinent through Arattupuzha Velayudha Panicker (AVP)

notionpress
.com

# The Leftover

A Relook on the Leftover Buddhist in the Indian Subcontinent through Arattupuzha Velayudha Panicker (AVP)

Rajan P Guruvanshy

notionpress.com

**Notion Press**

Old No. 38, New No. 6
McNichols Road, Chetpet
Chennai - 600 031

First Published by Notion Press 2016


ISBN 978-81-7511-079-3

# Contents

# Prologue

Indians still carry their stamps on them. *Caste, subcaste, group, subgroup, below poverty line, above poverty line, the poor, the so far unreached*, and so on are a few terms currently used by the powerful to place a stamp on them. In spite of a variety of empowerment and social reengineering programs, real empowerment can be seen in India among those wielding power. It has, of course, spread to a great extent after independence through corruption and decentralization of power. Through these processes, a new set of powerful emerge. These powerful also follow the old tradition of stamping; however, they employ new techniques. The process still ensures the majority are similar to the earlier, less privileged people. As was evident during the bygone days, power is shared among blood relatives and sycophants. Only residues, if any, are thrown to the leftover.

Being a student of economics, teaching the subject and working in apex banks as an economist, I could observe the people in seven different states in the Indian Union. The majority of them are poor, and they still experience an inbuilt fear and shyness. The ruling class makes use of these factors for their convenience. People, in general, are unable to even dream about a better quality of life. In fact, to me, they appeared to be burdened with a millennium-old stamping and deprivation.

After retirement from service, I happened to hear about a social change agent, Arattupuzha Velayudha Panicker. He lived on a small *thuruth* (an island) in earlier Odanadu 150 years ago. This place is currently located in Alappuzha district in Kerala state. Arattupuzha Velayudha Panicker had a different cult. People in the *thuruth* say that he reflected the "true Indian culture," which was lost. I had observed traces of a similar culture in many pockets in the subcontinent. Thus, I felt the subject was worth probing. This book is a humble attempt on the same subject.

I'm familiar with survey research: collecting and collating data, analyzing them, drawing inferences and drafting reports. Writing a novel is new to me. Therefore, due to ignorance, I might have broken all conventions related to writing. I have observed people reading books while travelling, watching television at home; I have also observed youth going to theatres. I hope this subject attracts them. The story is narrated by a set of young researchers and takes the form of a travelogue. The researchers have their own sub-stories. The story of AVP is characterized by thrill, action and humor; it also addresses dynamic changes and the love, care and compassion that are much wanting in today's world. The product mix, I hope, is worthy enough to attract scriptwriters and filmmakers. If I could prompt a few such people to have a relook at our rich past, my purpose is served. Showcasing the Leftover's strength is my agenda.

I'm inspired by Amma, my mother.

# 1

# In the Train

I woke up on hearing the rocking of Bharathiya Rail. The great rocking activated each of the cells of my body. Its lateral jerks seemed like those of an agitated bull that was trying to throw me out from my berth.

I clung tight to the rexin-covered chain that was hanging from my middle berth as I travelled in the fast-moving New Delhi–Trivandrum Kerala Superfast Express. I looked at my watch. It was 6:35 in the evening. The red and orange light of the setting sun sneaked in through the thick glass window panes of the three-tier AC compartment.

Suddenly, a tinge of fear flashed into my nerve. *Where is Tina, my friend?*

I looked down at the lower berth, which she was supposed to be occupied. Two senior citizens in white kurtha-pyjama were sharing their valuable views on the Delhi Metro Train. One of them was a Sardarji with his neatly combed beard and hair tied into a knot on his head.

I looked at the opposite end and at the side berth. Their occupants were sleeping. My pulse rate increased. Sitting on my knees in the middle berth, I tried to look down, leaning to the maximum extent possible. With a lateral jerk, my hair got loose and it fell as a heavy mass in between the senior citizens, interrupting their discussion.

Both of them were surprised at the sudden appearance of a hair mass in front of them.

They appeared irritated, and the Sardarji looked at my eyes in rage.

I tried to tie my hair and with folded hands, said,

"Excuse me uncle, I'm really sorry."

The train jerked me left and right. With folded hands, I repeated,

"Sorry uncle, I was looking for my friend, Tina."

The Sardarji's face changed. A smile appeared on his face. Both of them laughed and hit their palms like cricket bowlers who were sharing their feelings on a hard-earned wicket.

They woke up their wives. They too were stunned to see my sitting position, with folded hands, flowing hair and my struggle to balance myself on my berth.

"Beta, you scared us. For a moment, I had the Dharshan of Kalima."

Sardarji uncle's face was mischievous, and his eyes sparkled.

Turning to the lesser built-up aunty, the Sardar uncle said, "Suseela, why don't you help her to tie her hair?"

Unlike south Indians, north Indians quickly make you their *beta and beti* (son and daughter) and treat you like their children.

I looked at Suseela aunty. She was of my mother's age and had a pleasant face like any other Punjabi aunts on Jawaharlal Nehru University (JNU) campus.

I smiled at her, showing her the *namasthe* sign. "No aunty. I'll do it myself," I said.

Suseela aunty pulled out her handbag from the lower berth, fished out a large-sized comb and gestured me to get down.

I pushed out my legs to find the side ladder. My loose pyjamas and short kurtha were comfortable for the safe landing.

I felt grateful to my Kochamma (dad's younger brother's wife) in JNU who had insisted on the need for me to wear dignified outfits. She had reminded me to avoid sarees and other inconvenient clothes while travelling. The sky blue pyjama and short kurta that I was wearing were her choice. I approached Suseela aunty.

She gestured me to sit facing the window.

Squeezing in, I looked at Sardar uncle. He was smiling and trying to adjust himself to accommodate Tina.

"Uncle, should I ask Tina to shift to the upper berth?" I asked.

The idea impressed Suseela aunty and she said, "Pushpa, will you be interested in coming down?"

Pushpa aunty was waiting for the opportunity.

Suseela aunty stood up. She was moderately built and was perhaps in her late fifties.

"Aroraji, will you please help Pushpa to climb down, so that we can fold the middle berth?"

Tina got up and quickly reached the upper berth. A few bags and a couple of folded bed sheets were there. She looked down and asked,

"Can I use the upper berth? It's convenient for me."

She kept the luggage on one side, stretched and made herself comfortable.

I helped them fold the middle berths and ensured we were comfortable for a nice evening siesta.

The sun had almost set. I tried to have a glimpse of it through the window glass, but I could see only red dim lights and distant clouds through the long stretches of harvested fields. When I had first travelled towards north India, I had wondered why such long stretches of fields didn't have a vegetative cover as seen in Kerala.

Suseela aunty combed my hair entirely, taking out each knot with the skill of an expert. My hair was long, and most of the strands were as long as my knees. My mother insisted on my using only the oil she had made and had given this to me in small bottles. Probably the oil or my luck resulted in the air and water in Delhi being friendly to me during the last two years of my stay at JNU.

Sensing the peculiar smell of my hair, Suseela aunty parted it into two and asked, "Beta, can I make two plaits?"

I nodded and sat in such a way that she would feel comfortable. I could see the uncles on the dark glass of the train.

We ladies have a special skill to observe things happening around us. Suseela aunty showed her skill in handling my unruly hair.

Parting the hair on the left, Suseela aunty asked my name. I replied, "Chippy," and she laughed as if she had heard "papy."

"What is the meaning of Chippy?"

"Seashell," I replied.

"Bindraji, do you know the meaning of Chippy?"

Both the uncles exchanged clues and looked at Suseela aunty.

"This girl's name is Chippy, *maane* (viz), seashell." She added, "Perhaps she is coming from a hamlet near the sea. That's why her parents named her seashell." She smiled with gratitude at her scholarship.

Occasionally, I could see lights at a long distance. The train was travelling at peak speed, as if it wanted to reach the next station at the earliest.

"Beta, how come you are in Delhi?" It was Bindra uncle's voice. He called me beta like the *Dhooth Wala* (milkman) did in Kochachan's (father's younger brother) JNU staff quarters.

"I was in JNU and I have completed my M Phil in economics," I said. After a pause, I added, "My friend Tina is also doing her M Phil, but she is one year junior to me."

I tried to look at Bindra uncle with my detailed reply. But *auntyji* turned my neck to its original status.

We Indians have a curiosity to know more about other Indians. A hidden urge persuades us to know about the welfare of our fellow Indians.

"Are you two going to the same place? Are you related?" Aroraji asked. His curiosity might have perhaps arisen due to our different looks and our use of English as the common language.

"Tina is from Orissa, from a district called Malkangiri. She is joining me on vacation and will meet her parents in Bhubaneshwar after a week. In JNU, we share a room and we're friends."

"It is due to my constant requests that she is taking me to her home in Kerala," Tina shouted from the top berth.

I looked up. She was sitting and trying to put her legs down and swing them. Because of Suseela aunty's firm grip, I was unable to watch Tina's further movements.

"Beta, tell us about your home and village in Kerala." Bhindra uncle was curious.

"I'm from a poor family in Malkangiri," Tina was quick enough to respond. "My father is teaching in Bhubaneshwar in a higher secondary school, therefore I had my schooling there and then college education in a nearby town, Cuttak. Last year only, I joined JNU for M Phil," she said and looked down. I then got ready to supplement, based on requirement.

⁂

A mobile beeped, and Tina started looking for her mobile. Arora uncle traced it from the lower berth and handed it over to her. She looked at the phone and then at us. I was watching her on the window glass with the silent permission of Suseela aunty, who was almost finishing my second plait.

Holding the phone, Tina descended from the berth, like a teenage boy. She walked towards the toilet. I had been noticing her right from the time we left JNU. I knew she was hiding something from me. She ensured I was at a distance while she attended certain calls. I thought she must be having some issues with Arjun, her boyfriend hailing from Puri, who was working in the National Productivity Council, Delhi. They were engaged. *Why is this girl playing hide and seek?* I wondered.

I looked through the window. The last rays of the sun helped me visualize running objects. At a distance, I could also see the lights of a temple spreading down to the foothills.

Soon, all of us realized that our train had got onto a bridge as we heard its large and familiar "Tuck-dick, Tuck-dick, Tuck-dick" sound. Both the aunts quickly worshipped the mighty river beneath us. I looked down and could see only narrow silver lines reflecting the red sun rays. Suseela aunty abandoned my head, touched her own cheeks with synchronized movements and worshipped the river.

She fixed the comb on my hair, whispered a few lines saluting the Sath Gurus and touched her cheeks with both her hands. I tried to turn towards her. But she quickly ensured my posture was convenient to her and completed the second plait. She took out two rubber bands from her resource-rich handbag and tied the ends of each plait with her skill and strength.

Suseela aunty turned me towards the others and declared, "Now, Chippy's hair is safe till she reaches home." To the men, she added, "Doesn't she look like Rekha in *Khoob Soorath* (an old Hindi film)?"

The AC coach attendant moved in with bundles of small pillows, bedsheets and blankets. He looked at us and asked,

"All of you are to Kerala? Six sets, right? Where should I keep them?"

Bindra uncle gestured to the top berth on the ladies' side.

Tina rushed in and whispered, "Don't place an order for dinner. We have certain plans." Then, she left hurriedly.

My doubts were further strengthened. I wondered why there was so much of a hurry on a fast-moving train.

The railway caterer in uniform shouted, "Dinner, chapathi-chicken and vegetable meals, eight o' clock."

Arora uncle responded, "Not today." Turning towards me, he asked,

"Beta, have you brought anything for dinner?"

I was confused. "Tina will place the order," I replied awkwardly.

"Even if there is a problem, we shall accommodate you, beta." Bindra uncle stood next to me, making me feel comfortable.

The train appeared to be approaching a larger station. Its speed was decreasing. I looked at my watch. It was 7:40 in the night, and the lights on both sides indicated the proximity of a station. I tried to look out for some indication. However, I couldn't see any and so, I looked at Bindra uncle. He took out his railway guide. Referring the guide, he looked at his watch and said, "Beta, it is Bina."

I stood up and moved my neatly plaited hair in front—a nice job and one that only an expert can do, especially considering the limited space available on a running train! I thanked Sueela aunty and touched her feet. She stood up, held my face and kissed me on my forehead. I was unable to say anything. My eyes were wet and she helped me to turn my face towards Bindra uncle, who too tried to ease the situation.

The train came to a halt, and I tried to locate Tina. Once again, she was behaving like a boy. At the first chance, she jumped on to the platform and ran forward. Standing at the door, I leaned out to have a glimpse of her.

I walked to our slot. Suseela aunty looked at me, and her face reflected her concern.

"What is wrong? Are you OK?"

I said, "OK" and walked to her and whispered, "I am unable to locate Tina!"

She looked around and said in a low voice,

"She is not a child. She might be in the toilet and will be back soon."

Both the aunties shared my concern for Tina.

I was nervous and tried to look out through the window near the side seats.

It was occupied by a mother and her six-year-old son. Perhaps the child's father was the one who was sleeping on the side upper berth. Right from Delhi, he was found to be sleeping, turning his face towards the side of the train.

❋❋❋

Someone tapped on my shoulder. I turned and it was Tina with Arjun, her boyfriend!

I was shocked to see Arjun in the train. Tina never told me that he would join her during her trip to Kerala. All the others looked at Tina with a bit of agitation and anguish. Tina pulled me aside and whispered, "Arjun has joined us, and he will stay at Prof Bala's house. There are three boys and your Bala uncle will also reach home on Friday. He will fly from Delhi to Cochin. Arjun just told me this. Mrs Praful, working in Rail Bhavan, had arranged the tickets. But she couldn't get higher-class tickets. However, through her, we can expect some favors such as these dinner packets." She then showed me the hidden packets.

The train was about to move. Arjun got down hurriedly and shouted,

"Bye, I'll meet you tomorrow with certain items for breakfast." Since there was no vestibule to our compartment, he stepped out and ran towards the engine side of the train. I was unable to reconcile myself to the unexpected presence of Arjun.

My father is a friendly person. But I was unable to imagine Tina with her boyfriend around Mangalam village. It is an island with less than 800 families, and every one knows the other. An unknown boy and girl moving together in Mangalam will be hot news, and there will be many in our *thuruth* (island) who would be eager to watch this. Arjun is a cool guy, but Tina is a nut. If not controlled, she will create a "tsunami" there.

We moved to our bay. I briefed the uncles and aunties,

"She got down for collecting the dinner packets." I raised the carry bags, each containing a few aluminum packets, neatly packed.

I looked at my cell phone. There was not even a missed call. Before leaving the JNU campus, I had informed my father. Mom had also talked to me. They would be at Chengannoor railway station to receive us.

I looked at Tina. She was again busy with her cell phone, feeding a message. I was jealous. I had never expected to see Arjun in the train, and to hear that there were two more boys. One was Dr Praful, one of the seniormost scholars in Delhi University. I wondered who the other person was.

*What are they going to do in Mangalam? May be some work related to Bala uncle! I guessed.*

The Punjabi team was arranging for their dinner. I looked at Tina. She was still busy with her phone.

The bay was filled with Punjabi culinary smells. I couldn't prevent myself from salivating. Tina said, "Can we have our food?" Without waiting for an answer, she climbed upward with the water bottle and food packets.

Helping Tina, I told my local guardian, "We shall have dinner on the top berth."

Suseela aunty gave me a small *katori* (bowl) full of Punjabi pickles. We Indians enjoy sharing pickles and pappads, I thought.

I passed on the *katori* to Tina along with my water bottle and climbed upward.

Tina unpacked the aluminum foils and spread them on two newspapers. It was mutton biriyani, salad, pickle and curd.

Biriyani perhaps has its own story. It is said that Arabs brought it to India and the Mugal perfected it. From its smell, color and combination of the side dishes, I felt that the biriyani in front of us had some *Khaan Dhani* (family traditions) clout. It might have originated from a good restaurant in Bina.

"I know, you will kill me when we step down from the train at Chengannoor," Tina said avoiding eye contact.

"Believe me, I didn't know about Arjun's plan until we left the campus." Tina looked at my face, and she was trying to convince me.

"Look, it is your uncle's work. I guess there are serious things going on."

"I could gather from Arjun that there are three guys in the train and your uncle and family will also be at home during the weekend." She paused and added,

"Arjun is planning to return to Delhi by next Sunday along with the others. And, as you know, my ticket to Bhubaneshwar is also on the same day. But we have to travel in two different trains."

Tina was getting worried about my nonresponse. I was enjoying the good food. The biriyani tasted like the authentic

Mugal recipe. In between, the Punjabi pickles reminded me of a different palette of tastebuds, which was made to match with Punjabi perotta.

I remembered our cook Thomas in JNU hostel, who often displayed his skills with regard to Punjabi dishes in Kochamma's kitchen, especially at certain family parties that lasted until late in the night.

It was at such a party that I heard a mild roaring sort of a sound that captured the attention of about eight intellectuals of different ages who were sitting and enjoying the special dishes prepared by Thomas. Kochamma and her son didn't venture into such discussions. On that day, the strange voice was listened to by all, including Thomas. I stood behind the window curtain of the drawing room and listened. It resembled the sound of a Doordarsan English News reader in my school days.

He talked in a very low voice. But the group listened, and I was unable to see his face.

"If we had a Dark Age of more than a millennium, can we not search for its details?" Pausing for a moment, he said, "Our researchers are capable. Can't we seek institutional approval and attempt in-depth studies in a few selected regions?"

Kochamma came near to me and whispered,

"Now, it is interesting to listen. Neeraj has taken over."

Pulling me towards the kitchen, she said,

"Let us take our plates and sit at the window or the ladies can be in a group with them."

I was daydreaming!

"As usual, you are slow in eating." Tina looked at me, and I doubted her scanning eyes. Turning her cell phone towards me, she said,

"It is already 9:50 and our Punjabi team will switch off the lights by 10 o' clock."

I looked at Tina's dinner packet. It was empty.

"Would you like to have some more? I don't think I can do justice to Arjun's effort!"

Tina folded her hands and gestured that she was full and had no more space in her tummy.

I smiled and appreciated her quickness to finish a large meal. Tina looked at me and wanted to say something. I pretended ignorance on her preparations.

"Chippy, how far is your home from Prof Bala's?" Tina probed.

I could guess her mind. She was studying the possibility of her meeting Arjun, who would be staying with my uncle at our ancestral house. My house was about two kilometers away and it was near National Highway 47 (NH 47), connecting Kollam city with Alappuzha township. Every ten minutes, we got private buses and autorickshaw services were also available.

To prod me, she took little biriyani from my foil and pretended to help me in my difficulty. She waited for my reply. I chewed and enjoyed my food, and then I whispered,

"It may take half an hour by walk. We can also get the services of the boatmen to help us cross a half a kilometer wide river."

She was unconvinced. Looking dejected, she grumbled,

"How is your place different from Malkamgari, which you always call backward?"

Collecting her foil, she hurriedly climbed down and walked towards the wash area. I had a hearty laugh and focused myself on finishing my food at the earliest.

When I reached the wash area, Tina was standing towards the locked door and was looking for something on her cell phone.

Reaching nearer to her, I whispered, "Less than two kilometers. In private buses, you can reach within ten minutes."

I turned on the tap and washed my hands after pushing down the foils into the newly kept waste bin.

Hiding her curiosity, Tina enquired,

"In addition to your grandparents, who all are staying at your Mangalam house?"

She knew Prof Bala, my Kochachan, a faculty in JNU; and through me she had heard about my grandfather and grandmother. I called them *Achachan* and *Achamma.*

"During the vacations, you can expect atleast a visiting family," I said.

Of late, it has become a practice that in most of the ancestral houses in Kerala, there will be an assembly of close relatives, especially one's sons and daughters and their families who stay outside Kerala. Such an assembly happens especially during the summer vacation. It is an opportunity for the children to enjoy a few days with their grandparents and cousins. It also gives them an opportunity to run around, play, swim, observe the rural life and experiment with small adventures.

I have crossed that age, I thought. Perhaps, Tina may still fit in. She is childlike. When Arjun is around, she forgets the present.

Counting certain things with her left hand, Tina said,

"I'll be with you for six days." Looking at me, she continued,

"On the seventh day, I will board the train to Bhubaneshwar and will go with Arjun to New Delhi."

Holding my hand, she said, "I will return to JNU by the end of July and I'll miss you."

Tears spurted out in her beautiful eyes. Her palms were warm. The hot wind trying to get into the train reminded us of the extreme summer season even during night hours.

She said, "Our families are planning to arrange our marriage only after the submission of my dissertation."

"Why can't they arrange it during this vacation?" I asked. Without waiting for her reply, I added,

"Since Arjun is at Delhi, you can stay with him and he too will be able to help you to complete the project."

"Both of us are the eldest in our families. Our parents may have lots of expectations," Tina said, sharing her feelings. She added,

"Even for the engagement held at Bhubaneshwar, my pappa had to spend Rs. two lakhs in giving away gifts to close relatives, buying gold rings and paying for a small hotel at Nayapally in Bhubaneshwar. It was a small function that lasted less than two hours only. We chose Bhubaneshwar for the convenience of Arjun's family at Puri, so that they could reach Bhubaneshwar in an hour. Moreover, my parents had lived there for nearly twenty-three years and they have friends and relatives there, so we wanted them also to attend."

There was an increase in the number of co-passengers around the wash area, and we returned to our berths.

Both the uncles and aunties were trying to sleep, fighting the dim light. The upper berth was left for Tina, and the middle berth was left for me. Tina climbed up with her cell phone and water bottle.

I looked at Bindra uncle. There was no response. Perhaps the light was too dim for Bindra uncle to make out that I wanted to say goodnight to him.

I scampered to my middle berth. Once again, I was with the Bharathiya Rail. It rocked and often jerked me left and right, telling me that Chengannoor was far away. Gaining speed, the train started moving when we fell asleep.

I had an unusual faith in Bharathiya Rail and in the hundreds of her fast-running, long distance trains taking care of the thousands of passengers sleeping in her lap. For a moment, I felt immense love towards her caring drivers, guards, signal-giving staff, gangmen and the service-providing people. Their teamwork makes us sleep. There are always a few among us who are ready to take the responsibility and provide others with all comforts. It reminded me of Achachan's long tenure in the Southern Railway and of him retiring as an executive thirty-one years ago.

My thoughts slipped to Neeraj. Why is he so concerned about the Dark Age of India?

A 1,000-year-old untold story, he says. Why should a gold medalist of political science from Delhi University and a topper in the civil service examination be bothered about the Dark Age?

I wanted to see him talk. I had remembered Kochamma's praise of him.

"He is Neeraj Guptha, first-rank holder in the civil service examination, and he hesitated to undergo training at Mussoorie." She paused and added,

"Your Bala Kochachan and his friends persuaded him to attend the training."

That day, he was sharing his experience in Mussoorie. But the focus of the discussion happened to be more on the collective responsibility of the academician to carry out research work on the less known period.

Drawing the attention of Prof Saxena, Neeraj pleaded, "Sir, if a sizable number of Indians are still not included in the socioeconomic development process, is it not our responsibility to study the root causes, frame our policies at the grassroot level and empower them to participate?"

Thomas placed the steel vessels containing dinner items on the table.

Prof Bala preferred tandoori rotis with one vegetarian and one nonvegetarian curry. Only three to four items were usually served. Steel plates and a large jug containing chilled buttermilk were served as usual.

Thomas whispered to Prof Bala, waved at us and hurriedly left.

Such discussions took place once in a month. The assembly would be held in each participant's house on JNU campus in turns. Thomas the great would prepare simple dishes. He would also bring provisions after an assessment of the available items at home. All the ladies loved it, as they need not cook during such nights. Often, Thomas would also introduce a new item.

Around nine o' clock, Bala uncle's PhD scholars also joined: three boys and a girl. Prof Bala had invited them for dinner.

Wishing the gentlemen, Sunitha Sreevasthava came in, wished Kochamma and said "hallo" to me.

Kochamma was familiar with all scholars pursuing research under Prof Bala.

Sunitha collected the pickle and water bottles from the fridge and complimented Kochamma on her skill in making pickles.

Kochamma ensured the number of plates, glasses and spoons was correct for the group for the dinner.

She moved to the drawing room, invited the guests and called her son, Aswin who was in his study room.

Sunitha took initiative in introducing me to the group in the dining hall.

"Let us welcome the young scholar, Ms Chippy from Kerala. She is a student of economics and the pretty daughter of Prof Bala's elder brother…" She paused. Bala helped her, "Adv Satheesh Chandra Babu."

Smilingly, I said, "Hai."

"It appears that the family members of Prof Bala are unusually tall," Neeraj complimented me and then paused for an endorsement from Bala.

"Compared with our elders, we are pygmies," Bala said. He added, "My father is six feet, three inches and his great-grandfather, Arattupuzha Velayudha Panicker, I heard, was unusually tall and Homeric."

Neeraj was taller than me. His face looked tired, perhaps due to tiresome travel. In the backdrop of his unkept hair and two to three days of delayed shavings, he appeared wanting sleep.

Kochamma with Sunitha helped us form a women's group.

"Neeraj was our representative in the recently held Asian student meet at Kuala Lumpur."

Looking at me, Sunitha said,

"He is also pursuing his PhD under Prof Saxena, and therefore, wanting a placement in Delhi after his training."

Smiling at Sunitha, Neeraj moved near to the elders who had already formed a small circle with the available chairs. Drawing a chair, Neeraj joined the group.

I wanted to sit near Neeraj. Kochamma managed two chairs, and she and Sunitha sat near Prof Bala.

I looked around and saw a few plastic stools stacked in one corner. I arranged them just behind Neeraj and requested the remaining research scholars to make themselves comfortable.

Once they took their seats, I took mine and sat just behind Neeraj, so that I could hear just him.

The discussions revolved around the missing links during the Dark Age and the participation of researchers from neighboring countries in unearthing the truth.

Drawing the attention of the group, Neeraj said,

"With the help of selected neighboring universities, can we study the social history for a specific period, say 100 years, for a specific region and evolve methods to study the missing links?"

He added, "Even within a region, there can be a wide variety of information, knowledge and skill that is worth documentation. The most important among these can be listed out and documented based on the availability of resources and time. In-depth studies can be further carried out. Internet can be used to disseminate such information and for arriving at a consensus."

I whispered my views to the scholars sitting close to me.

Turning to our side, Neeraj said,

"Saxena ji let us hear the new scholars. They may have some plausible suggestions."

All of them looked at us, and the two research scholars sitting with me also looked at me to start talking. I was in a fix. Neeraj encouraged me,

"Come on Chippy, you were saying something." Then, he paused.

It was an opportunity, and my pappa had trained me to grab it.

"Can we develop a blog on a prioritized subject, invite views from worldwide and build a team of researchers with similar interests?"

In one breath, I blabbered and looked at Sunitha for help.

But, no one from our group supported me. Praful, sitting opposite me, said,

"With the help of the Internet, we may be able to draw the attention of researchers who are interested in collaborative work."

Subsequently, Sunitha took over. She explained,

"Multidisciplinary research is in the nascent stage and if JNU initiates, we shall be pioneers in tracing the Dark Age within our subcontinent."

Looking at Prof Saxena and Prof Bala, she added "Our South Asian neighbors and China, perhaps, will share valuable information that would help us bridge the missing links."

I felt comfortable and wanted Neeraj to look at us. But he didn't. Instead, Prof Saxena said,

"Can we initiate a multidisciplinary research project, seek the support of the Indian Council for Social Science Research (ICSSR) and encourage a couple of our M Phil students to shortlist topics that are of common interest among the likely participating two or three neighboring countries?"

I was happy and looked at Kochamma. She smiled and looked at her husband. He was silent. He was like that, always hesitant to uplift me. May be he was right. One should fight for survival. That's enjoyable.

A murmur from our side broke the silence. After a hectic exchange of ideas, Neeraj shared our views,

"Shall we form a small team of two to three young scholars with Saxena Sahib as guide and project coordinator?"

Without losing time, the team emerged under Prof Saxena with Praful, Alex, Sunitha and me. Alex was a Sri Lankan, a student of economics who had just submitted his thesis in Delhi University for the award of PhD.

Neeraj looked at me and whispered, "Are you happy?"

I was unable to hide my joy and moved closer to him and whispered, "thank you."

I wanted to say many more things to Neeraj. The nearness to him gave me a magical feeling of gaining something unexpected. I wished the discussion would continue. But the group members looked at their watches, and a couple of them stood up to leave.

Prof Saxena called us nearer to him and said,

"Each one of you prepare a brief write-up, discuss among yourselves and we shall finalize the strategy next week."

Turning to Praful, the seniormost among us, he said,

"You will coordinate the project activities." He paused and said,

"goodnight" and then he left with the others.

I followed Bala uncle to see them off and walked up to the gate. It was 10:50 in the night, and all were in a hurry to reach their home or hostel.

I looked at Neeraj. He might stay with someone in Delhi. Where will he stay? I thought.

He was with Praful, as a pillion rider on his bike. Perhaps, he would stay with him in the research scholars's hostel or in Poorvanchal or Brahmaputhra, the popular boys' hostel in JNU. But I didn't know where Praful stayed.

Praful was kick starting the bike and Neeraj shouted,

"Bala Sab, I'm leaving for Mussoorie next Sunday and will meet you all during the week." He paused and looked at us, waved goodbye and left.

In the study room, a small cot was kept for Bala uncle's relaxed reading. I preferred to sleep on it. Kochamma gave me a pillow and a quilt. It was the first week of November. Mornings in Delhi during those days were chilly, especially when one wants to enjoy Sundays.

My cell phone beeped for the first time after the sun had set. It was Bala uncle's call.

"Hello Chippy, where have you reached?" He paused and enquired, "Are you all ok?"

Without waiting for my reply, he continued,

"*Chettai* (elder brother) called me just now. They are unable to contact you over phone!"

I said, "I too tried but failed. We have left Bina and there is a Punjabi family with us travelling to Kanyakumari. They are helpful and we are safe."

I wanted to ask about his travel plans. But I didn't. He said,

"Chippy, we all will be there on Friday. We shall be there for a week only. I thought our boys can also have a break at Mangalam these days. They were longing to see *Achan* (father). He too likes to spend time with the youth, you know."

He paused and wanted to listen to me. But our loving Bharathiya Rail took us to another long bridge and I shouted,

"Kochacha, will you please call pappa and tell him that we are ok?" Saying this, I hung up.

I looked down. All were sleeping. I wondered how much of time I had spent with Neeraj.

It all happened just now, I felt. I longed to meet him and counted down the days in JNU hostel. On one Friday evening, I reached Kochachan's Dakshinapuram residence for a change.

As usual, on Saturday early morning, both Kochachan and his wife were getting ready to visit the Hanuman Temple at R. K. Puram.

Kochamma was regular in her Saturday visits to Hanuman Temple. They would return by 9:30 in the morning after having their breakfast at their favorite restaurant and would bring a food packet for their son, Aswin, and me.

Kochamma confirmed and said that Aswin was still sleeping.

Walking to the car, she added, "In case he wakes up, give him a glass of warm milk. Also tell him that mum will bring *Chola-Battura*, his favorite dish from the Punjabi dhaba."

The car was slowly moving out. Kochamma ran towards the gate. Joining her, I whispered,

"Today, I too want *Chola-Battura.* Please bring their *Achar* (pickle) and curd, the large cup. It would be a fine match."

Closing the gate, I came in. I had to wait for another three long hours for the Battura. Aswin is not dependable. He will wake up and run to play cricket with his friends. He is a typical Delhi brat. He eats a lot, plays a lot and surprisingly he is also good at his studies. His sister, Sunitha, is almost eight years older than him and she is a final year MBBS student in JIPMER, Pondicherry. We call her *Suni*, and she always had a complaint that Aswin never gives her company. He doesn't like girls, especially sisters. The last time, I wanted him to share the Kerala speciality *Appam* and egg curry that Kochamma had brought for me as well as Aswin's *Chola-Battura.* But he said a flat "no." Both his parents tried to persuade him to share with me. But he didn't budge.

I wanted to hit him. But I didn't. My brother Sidharth can be easily cajoled. He is in his first year of graduation in engineering and he likes girls. Suni is his favorite. When she is at Mangalam, my brother, Sidharth, will be with her. She moves on his bike to the nearby town, visits malls, watches cinema and also visits relatives. She loves to spend her vacation at Mangalam. On such days, Sidharth stays with her. Both of them share a good resemblance.

I'm a bit different. My pappa often says that in terms of looks only I am like Suni. Otherwise, I'm like my Ammamma, mom's mother. I have seen her only in photos and in a large painting in mom's house at Cochin.

I went to Aswin's room. He was sleeping like a pig. He was only thirteen, but five feet, three inches tall and weighed more than sixty-five kilograms. I wanted to give him a kick. Why can't he be a younger brother to me? He loves only his high-energy friends, the Delhi brats.

What should I do? I thought of taking an elaborate bath, shampooing and conditioning my hair.

The tubewell water was warm. Since it was early morning, I could enjoy a warm shower. With the help of the traditional shampoo that my Achamma (father's mother) had given me, I washed my hair.

With the dryer that I had found in Kochamma's room, I dried my hair. I also used her traditional smoking device with *Kundirikam* and a mixture of other herbal condiments prepared by Achamma.

The room was filled with fragrant smoke. It was also a bit choking. I took it to the open space attached to the bedroom, spread my hair on a nearby chair and placed the smoker plate on the floor. I drew a small stool and made myself comfortable. The well-cropped hedges of *Mehandi* gave me good privacy. I could also rest assured of a good view of the front gate. The morning sun rays warmed up the hedges. Tiny birds sat on them and spread their wings to keep themselves warm.

❋❋❋

To my surprise, the doorbell rang. I went nearer to the railings of the balcony, leaned myself over and asked, "who is there?"

I was frozen to see Neeraj. He too was surprised to see me wrapped in a towel and with my hair spread out.

"Good morning Chippy. I'm sorry to reach so early. There is an urgency and I want to talk to you."

I was like a robot for a moment. I reached the drawing room, unlocked the front door and said,

"Just a minute, I will change and come soon. Please be seated."

Handing over the newspaper to him, I smiled and moved into the study room, picked up my bag and took out my best available dress. I tied up my hair with the help of the wet towel, put on a *bindi* available on the dressing mirror of Kochamma and went towards Neeraj.

I tried to be normal. But sweat spurted out on my forehead. Wiping it, I switched on the fan and said,

"Prof Bala and Mrs Bala have gone to Hanuman Temple." Looking at Aswin's room, I uttered,

"He is sleeping. I just finished my bath and you arrived."

I glanced at him. He was fresh and handsome.

He smiled and said,

"I have seen Prof Bala and his wife going out. It is Saturday, and my expectation was right. I wanted to meet you." He looked into my eyes.

I was unable to look anywhere other than into his loving eyes. Those eyes wanted to tell me something. I knew them for ages, I felt.

I wanted to have a support and leaned on to the wall nearby.

He kept the newspaper on the center table, walked nearer to me and in a quivering voice whispered,

"Do you like me?"

I was unable to answer. I covered my face with both my hands, and the wall supported me.

He repeated, "Chippy, do you like me?"

That sound was nearer to me. My body warmed up in an unusual chemistry. I wanted to hear it again and again. Like a robot, I stamped my left foot vigorously on the floor and showed my impatience.

I'm unable to express those moments in words. I folded my hands very closely on my face, stamped my foot like a machine and stopped to listen again.

There was total silence, except his breathing and the flow of warm air that fell on my face.

The conquering voice again whispered,

"Chippy, do you like me? I want to marry you."

I was unable to breathe and even to look at him. I stamped both feet, one after the other, in an unusual rhythm.

Neeraj caught hold of my wrist and looked at my face. My eyes were closed. Our breathing was one and the same.

"Chippy, look at me. I want an answer." He paused and asked,

"Do you love me?"

I looked into his eyes. They were in doubt. Pushing him, I said,

"Stupid. Why do you ask me such silly questions?"

My eyes filled with the finest tears of love.

They gave him a readymade reply.

"I was waiting for ages to hear this from you."

I was unable to hide my feelings. I could feel his smell and the undisturbed surrounding.

Neeraj took my face into his hands and kissed my permissive, wet eyes.

I looked into his eyes and closed them for him. He read my warm lips and sealed them with his possessiveness.

I wanted to be his for the moment, for all the moments to come and to stay melted in his arms.

It was his own chemistry that enabled him to withdraw, and he took the chair with the newspaper in his hands.

Realizing the situation, I offered, "Would you like to have a cup of coffee?"

I added, "I too want it."

Without waiting for the reply, I moved to the kitchen.

"Wait for a moment," the loving voice said, echoing in the room,

"What were the Kuchupudy like steps that you were engaged in doing?"

I blushed and turned towards him. My naughty nature enabled me to instantaneously mimic those steps, and he burst into laughter.

I could see him struggling to control his laughter with both his hands.

I went to Aswin's room. Thank God, he was still sleeping. For the first time in my life, I felt him to be my little, cute brother.

I wanted to kiss him on his cheeks like the *Didis* do in the television ads.

Placing the milk and the water mix on the gas stove, I looked for Neeraj.

He was not in the drawing room. I could locate him in the verandah in one of the three chairs kept for visitors.

I had a hidden smile at the bottom of my belly. These boys are class-one thieves, I felt.

He trespasses the house with meticulous planning and robs the family's most valuable asset with her consent.

It is worth to be researched. Such a thief, after stealing the heart, reads the newspaper, sitting right in front of the house!

Beware of such thieves! My heart warned itself, as if I were not a partner in what happened!

Our hearts are like that, I felt, and, the coffee tasted better than ever before.

I fell in love with Kochamma's filter coffee, which I could use for Neeraj. She is proud of her skill to make filter coffee. It was inherited from her father, who was a branch manager in Bank of Baroda in Coimbatore. A senior officer's mother hailing from Mylapore in Chennai had taught him her family secret of making wonderful filter coffee.

I thanked the entire lineage for enabling me to make an excellent large cup of coffee for the great thief posing as Raja Harichandra, the mythological king who never uttered a lie.

I kept the mugs of coffee on the table and sat opposite to Neeraj.

He looked at me and his eyes scrolled down. To come out of the scanning, I asked,

"What would you like to have for breakfast?"

He looked into my eyes again, took the coffee mug and whispered,

"Yes, Chiklu."

"What?" I said.

"Yes, my favorite Chiklu," he giggled.

I was curious. I had never heard of a breakfast called Chiklu!

May be something related to Guptha's in Bulandshare relish, I thought.

With a student's curiosity, I asked, "How it is made?"

He looked at me and said,

"It is already made for me. You just sit before me, I'll enjoy my breakfast."

His eyes rolled on my eyes and lips.

I took my mug and mimicked as though I was throwing the content to quench his thirst.

I looked at Neeraj's watch. It was 9:15 in the morning. It was time for them to return.

I wished the Punjabi dhaba providing Chola-Batoora for Aswin had a long queue today.

Immediately, it struck me. Can we have one more set of chola-batoora for the thief too?

I ran to the study, picked up my cell and contacted Kochamma.

They were at Kochamma's favorite Tamil restaurant. I briefed her,

"Neeraj is waiting to meet you both and likes to have breakfast. He too wants chola-batoora with all accompaniments."

I was happy. Now, they will reach here, only after half an hour. And I am safe, by informing them of Neeraj's presence at home.

I felt proud of my quick intelligence and went to Aswin's room and woke him up.

I lured, "my little cute python, there is chola-batoora especially for you today. Pappa and mamma are coming with the Punjabi dhaba kits. Get up and brush your teeth on your own. Neeraj *Chetan* (brother) will give you company."

He jumped out of his bed and looked for Neeraj. Neeraj waved and said,

"Good morning Aswin. I heard it is chola-batoora for breakfast."

He reciprocated, "Hai Neeraj *Bhaiya* (brother), perhaps Chippy *Didi* (*elder sister*) is cheating us. It may be her latest bluff."

I showed him my cell phone and said,

"Just now, I talked to your mama. They are at the Tamil restarant at R. K. Puram and soon will be at your Punjabi dhaba. Do you want to talk to them?" I offered my phone to him.

He felt convinced.

"What you have asked for?"

"The same chola-batura and curd,"

He looked at me first and then at Neeraj and enquired,

"How many sets you have asked for?"

"Three. One for you and one each for Neeraj and I."

He was still having a doubt and whispered,

"I'm not going to share with any," and he walked towards the toilet.

I looked at Neeraj and he indicated a thumbs-up sign.

I shouted at Aswin, "You brush, take your bath and join us. I'm keeping your milk on the dining table" and then, I walked to the verandah.

Neeraj was unable to hide his laugh. He struggled and said,

"You look simple, but a hard nut." He looked at me with his mischievous eyes.

It is fun to look at him in such a mood.

He looked like a mischievous boy impatient to do many things.

I wanted to prick him and asked,

"How have you topped the civil service exam?"

I kept my chair at a safer distance and looked at the gate in between.

He wanted to bite me and answer my question. For a moment, I felt, I could lock him in his chair. My cute lion was caged. I looked at his eyes and turned my right thumb, imitating the neck movement of a dancer.

He wanted to catch me with the skill of a cricketer, put me into his pocket and hit me like the great Sachin Tendulkar exhibits his hidden feelings on the long harassed bowler in a world cup match.

I could successfully cage the lion cub right in front of me.

Often, I looked at the gate. My gestures were enough to keep him confined in the chair. He was restless. He wanted to grab me and throttle me with his deep kisses.

I could read the synopsis on his face. Through my eyes, I could force him to place them before the select committee.

***

I ran towards the gate and opened it.

Kochamma got down with three separate polythene bags of the famous Punjabi dhaba. Grabbing them, I closed the gate and ran towards Aswin.

I wanted to see myself in a mirror. I felt something more in me and wanted to tune it down.

Giving one packet to Aswin and leaving the other two on the dining table, I went to the toilet and closed it. I checked my face and dress.

I wondered whether my lips were unusually red. I looked at them. The mirror in the toilet could not clarify my doubt. I tied my hair properly with the help of the towel and came out.

Kochamma was helping Aswin to have his favorite dishes in a plate.

I helped her to arrange the dining table and asked,

"Shall I prepare coffee for you too, so that we can be together at the dining table?"

Kochamma smiled and nodded in affirmation. I wanted to buy some more time to make myself normal. Poor Neeraj was left alone with the newspaper and Bala uncle was in his room, perhaps changing into his favorite mundu and kurta.

I was still in the kitchen and Kochamma invited Neeraj into the dining hall and said,

"We had breakfast and it is for you three. Chippy is making coffee."

She came inside the kitchen and whispered,

"Go and join Neeraj. Bala may take time," and she took charge of the coffee making.

I looked at Neeraj. He was not comfortable. I took a seat near to him and said,

"Chola-battura is Aswin's favorite."

And we looked at Aswin. He was too busy relishing the food. But we also felt that he was watching us.

Quite unexpectedly, Neeraj stamped on my toe. I withdrew my leg and slipped into hiccups. I murmured "sorry" and moved to the wash basin. To my surprise, I noticed the missing *bindhi* on my forehead and walked towards Neeraj, forgetting the hiccups. Silently, I looked for the *bindhi* on my towel. I looked at Neeraj and indicated the missing *bindhi*.

Neeraj too silently searched for the *bindhi*. But his face reflected his helplessness. I came and sat near Aswin with my plates and shared a batura with him.

Without looking at me, he murmured,

"Buttering me with batura?"

Changing his voice, he mimicked Mohanlal, the versatile Malayalam cine-actor.

"Mone Dinesha, a thousand Baturas will not be sufficient to keep the secret."

I got irritated.

"What secret? Who do you think, you are?" I pricked his ear.

"What is the problem? What made you both brother and sister to open up the latest world war?"

As usual, his voice reverbed in the hall.

Aswin washed his hands and pulled out his cricket bat from the corner box and walked towards Neeraj. Though he was only thirteen, he was huge. I was nervous and watched his movement. There was a flash of fear on Neeraj's face too.

Bending to Neeraj, he kept his hand on Neeraj's shoulder, in a super quick movement pulled out something, walked towards me, pasted on my forehead and once again mimicked Mohanlal,

"*Mone Dinesha, nee kuttiyanu* (You're a child). You seek permission from Achan, Achachan and even from late AVP."

Bending his shoulders, he winked at Neeraj and walked out in Mohanlal's style.

Neeraj stood up with a firm face. He shouted,

"Aswin, please stop."

He moved nearer to him, touched his feet in typical north Indian style and whispered,

"Boss! Please bless us."

Changing the bat from left to right hand, Aswin posed as Hanuman Maharaj (Hindu God) with his *gadha,* kept his right hand on Neeraj's head and said aloud,

"*Ayushmanbhav,* Take care. Take care of yourself."

He paused, looked around and whispered,

"Take care of my sister too"; stylishly, he walked out, flashing the bat from left to right and from right to left hand.

After a few steps, he turned back to me and winked.

I was furious. I could lay my hands only on the empty steel tumbler and I threw it at him in full force, which he skillfully knocked down with his bat.

I ran towards him forgetting everything. I could catch him near the gate.

I caught hold of his collar and gave him half a dozen hits on his back. He bent and allowed me to hit at my best, as if nothing was happening to him.

I left him and gasped for my breath. He looked at me with the most mischievous eyes. I was unable to bear them anymore. I clung to him and kissed him on both cheeks and his forehead.

"What is that *thamasa* (fun) at the gate?" It was Kochachan's stubborn voice. We turned and saw all the three walking towards us.

Aswin picked up my towel from the ground and put it on my shoulder. He pushed me towards them and ran out of the campus, throwing his bat high up in the air and catching the same.

"What is going on?" Kochachan repeated. Kochamma was stunned to see the crumpled towel that was full of sand.

It was Neeraj who came to my rescue. He said,

"It's the world wide war wherein there is no space for peacemakers."

He paused, smiled at Bala and said,

"They fight and they find peace. That is what we could witness."

Kochamma took away the wet towel and went towards the bathroom.

I was in a fix. I collected and put my hair in front of me, slowly walked and crossed them. The moment I crossed, I ran for my life towards the study.

It was the happiest day in my life.

I had got Neeraj and I had also got my Aswin, the devil.

Both of them are nuts who are blessed with good genes.

They could make me a joker. And the joker loved them.

The fast-running Kerala Express only listened to my story. All others slept.

Even Bindra uncle slept.

I looked at the cell phone. It was midnight. The AC was perfectly working. I pulled up the blanket along with the inner white sheet.

***

I don't know whether I slept or not. Kochamma called and said, "Neeraj is leaving for Mussoorie."

I jumped out and followed Kochamma like one of the most obedient and innocent school girls on earth.

Neeraj was standing outside the house with Prof Bala. I wanted to see him off. I wanted to atleast cling on to his hand till we reached the gate. But I unwillingly kept myself behind Kochamma. There was an unusual shyness in me that prevented me from looking at Neeraj.

What wrong did he do to me?

But I couldn't help myself from hiding behind Kochamma.

The car moved out of the gate. I ran behind the car and waved at Neeraj, who looked out and waved at me.

The car faded out of my sight. I stood still waving.

Kochamma tapped on my shoulder and said,

"You concentrate on your studies and finish the course at the earliest."

That is what I did. And I'm alive in Kerala Express. No one is with me. I'm alone. That Neeraj, stupid, idiot and male chauvinist, did not even telephone me.

No…No…He had called once and advised,

"Chiklu, will you please complete your program within the shortest time?"

All these guys advise. India is famous for its advisers.

That is what I did for the bastard. Each day I was spending on an average twelve hours and completed my project assignments before time. Why would I score A+ in all internals if I don't love that cub?

Man doesn't know how a woman loves him!

Can't he telephone me atleast once in a week?

Where is he now? And what is he doing? I don't know.

What he is digging in Mussoorie?

I think Bala uncle and his family wanted to pack me from JNU and safely dump me in my home.

What is my achievement, an M Phil in economics from JNU? With that, I may get a teaching job in one of the nearby colleges in Alappuzha or Kollam district. After a year, another lecturer or a professional will marry me and my life will be like any woman's life in a small town in Kerala.

But I wanted to be different. But I don't know how I can attain this?

That is why I envy Neeraj. He is different.

Where is he? Should I call him at midnight and give him a threat from the fast-running Kerala Express or unload the *gaalies* (bad words) I learned from JNU?

Today is the fourth day after the completion of my assignments in JNU. I sent a message on that very day when I completed them.

And the reply came after three long hours.

"Chicklu, don't worry. I'll meet you soon."

Is he so miserly? Neeraj Guptha and his *Khandhan* (family) might be one of the *Kanjoos* (misers) in Bulandshare.

One day, I planned to visit Bulandshare, his native town, and to walk into his home on the pretext of a census data enumerator. That nutty Tina only stopped me telling that members of his family would be clever enough to weed me out and some time, I may end up in the police station.

In India, nobody cooperates, especially on innovative work. We are slaves. During only those Buddhist times, we were fearless. Even our unity today is through fear only.

Why should I think all these things in Kerala Express? I turned, curled myself in her lap and she stroked me to an eternal motherly bliss.

❦❦❦

Someone woke me up. I looked at my cell phone. It was 10:40 in the morning. I was shocked to see the encroached summer rays in our AC cabin. I looked down. I was on the top berth and remembered that some time ago Tina had asked me to move to the upper berth.

I felt fresh. Once again, I looked down and Suseela aunty smiled and gestured me to get down.

I saw Bindra uncle reading the newspaper, *Madhya Pradesh (MP) Chronicle*. Perhaps the train might have crossed Madhya Pradesh and was nearing Warangal, one of the major stations in Andhra Pradesh.

My hair was intact. I arranged it and with my handkerchief cleaned my face and got down.

As usual, Tina was not around. In the lower berth, Arora aunty was lying and Arora uncle too was busy with a share of the *MP Chronicle*.

I said "good morning," bowed to Bindra uncle and searched for my sandals.

I reached near the toilet area and saw Tina and Arjun standing near the closed door and engaged in creamy talk.

Seeing me, Tina said,

"I'm hungry. He brought breakfast at 9:00 in the morning. It is nearing eleven now. Why don't you hurry so we can have breakfast?"

I smiled at Arjun, gave a wooden face to Tina and slammed the toilet door.

By luck, it was clean.

May be the railway staff had cleaned the toilet at the earlier station.

We passengers spoil them, and the railway staff punishes us.

We are yet to build a partnership for the convenience of both. From the current mutual harassment, we have to build a culture consisting of mutual help and enjoyment.

The morning was pleasant and I can wish anything, I thought.

It is free India. We can be free to spoil the toilet too.

It is also a way to celebrate our freedom. We all love to express ourselves, and our culture is reflected even in our toilets.

My thought process enabled me to leave the toilet clean.

Seeing me, Arjun and Tina posed as if they were waiting for me.

We joined the Punjabi lobby, and Tina took the lead in arranging the breakfast.

"Beta, you had an excellent sleep, I suppose." It was Bindra uncle's voice.

Arranging and acknowledging the skill of his wife behind my tied-up hair, I said,

"Uncle, yesterday, I wanted to say goodnight to you, may be at 10:30, but you were in deep sleep."

"Did you hear his snoring?" Suseela aunty exclaimed, and she looked at the uncles.

"I didn't," I said, and joined our breakfast group.

"No beta, I snore only when Suseela wakes up." He looked at me and added,

"It's deliberately done, so that I can sleep hearing the household chorus that is friendlier than her snoring!"

Arora uncle's loud laughter made the bay vibrant.

Arora aunty too joined. Arjun looked at Suseela aunty and he struggled to hide his laughter in his mouth filled with food. His eyes bulged and he left the bay.

"Both of them snored through their entire life. But they have two boys, that too twins. They are thirty years or older." It was Aroraji's contribution, and Bindra uncle cracked,

"I'm sure that I wasn't sleeping and snoring, at least at that time."

Bindra aunty took the *MP Chronicle*, the easy available weapon near her, and beat her husband on his head and shoulders. He defended the familiar attacks with the most mischievous moves.

Punjabis love jokes. They have a skill to make jokes and crack them in the right context and to read between the lines.

The JNU campus is a den of jokes; both good and dirty. Sometimes, even a serious discussion ends up in a joke and the group enjoys it.

❋❋❋

The breakfast was very good. The packet contained *aloo-ka-parota*, mango pickle and a small cup of neatly sealed fresh curd. Licking my fingers, I looked at Arjun in appreciation and gestured *adipoly* (superb).

"God is taking care of us. You simply enjoy." He announced this like the immobile DD news reader.

I looked at Tina. But she was with her food like the lone cub chewing a chicken leg.

The train indicated signs of nearing a station. Arjun, with the help of the boy sitting on the side seat, tried to locate it.

I wrapped up my breakfast foils, moved to the washbasin and called Arjun by gesturing to him.

"Tell me who all are travelling with you?" I asked in a firm voice.

"They are from Delhi University. You know Dr Praful. Along with him there is a senior scholar, Alex, from Sri Lanka. You might have seen him at your uncle's JNU quarters along with other research scholars. He had taken keen interest in arranging the visit program."

He looked at me and added, "Praful's wife is in Indian Railway Service (IRS); with her help, we got the reservation and she had arranged the food as well."

It was convincing, I felt. I was unable to control my curiosity and said,

"Arjun, do they have any specific project in mind? Can I also fit in?"

"No, they are planning something else. The present visit is only to see your grandfather as per Prof Bala's guidance and spend a few days with him for gathering basic information about the area where the ancient Buddhist abode Sreemoolavasom thrived."

He paused and added,

"I gathered that the Department of History in Delhi University is trying to submit a project on a subject related to our ancient culture for the consideration by the UNESCO."

Arjun is a statistician and perhaps, he does not know details.

"Do you have any idea about the research teams' stay?" Tina was curious.

"Would you like to join them?" I smiled and asked.

"They plan to spend some time with Bala's father and finalize their future plans. That's what I could gather from their talks," Arjun said.

"Can we stay together at one place?" Tina was again curious.

It was her wish. She wanted to ensure Arjun's presence around her.

"You have come to Kerala to stay with me at our home, not in the ancestoral home in Mangalam!" I reminded her.

"Oh, no, I like to move as a team with your grandfather and visit places, meet people and listen to him. I think it is fun and all of us will enjoy."

Tina looked at me and Arjun and posed as if she was the only one concerned about our welfare.

"I want to be with my pappa and mom at my home. It is vacation and both of them will be at home. My brother will also join after a week. How can I leave them and stay with you at Mangalam?"

Arjun got convinced. He nodded his head in favor of me.

"Your pappa and mom can also join us at Mangalam. Then the problem can be solved."

Tina explored the possibility of not getting out of Mangalam.

I couldn't check her entry to the Mangalam house along with Arjun. She meticulously planned to stay at Mangalam in the company of Arjun and decided to stump me out.

I joined the Punjabi team, leaving Tina and Arjun at the wash area.

I saw Khushwanth Singh's *Collection of Jokes* with Arora uncle. I borrowed it and withdrew to the upper berth.

The book could find a joker in me too. I felt jealous of Tina and failed to concentrate on the book.

Why should I feel jealous of her? That Neeraj fellow has made me a fool. His training might be already over? Or did he run away from Mussoorie?

He is capable of doing such things. What is so great about him when he has not tried contacting me? I'm lonely in a train, and he should have realized the same.

Even Bala uncle kept Neeraj away from me for the past one year. What went wrong? My pulse rate increased.

Are these guys troubleshooters?

My mom used to say that those boys and girls scoring very high grades in exams are problematic. She loves students with average scores and keeps them away from the extra smart.

I wanted to be with my mom and dad. I could smell my mom and in seconds I was within her fold.

❋❋❋

Tina woke me up and said, "It is 4:30 in the evening. You are yet to have your lunch. The packet Arjun brought is hanging there," she said, pointing towards the railway hooks.

I am comfortable with my loving mom and pappa and whispered,

"I'll have them for my dinner," and I hid myself in Kerala Express and pulled up the white sheet.

Stepping down from the middle berth, Tina murmured,

"Now she will get up tomorrow morning at Chengannur."

I felt happy to be with myself, with my parents and in Kerala Express. After leaving home, I was never so close to them. It's wonderful. I enjoyed myself.

The hectic activities below woke me up.

I looked down and saw the Punjabi team with Tina and Arjun making themselves comfortable for dinner.

I looked at my lunch packet. It was hanging there safely. I looked down and said,

"Arjun, do you have anything special for dinner?"

"Our extra care with regard to food supplies ended at Vijayawada. Now it's sarkari dinner with the added courtesies of Suseela aunty," Tina murmured.

Looking up, she added, "For you, food is saved here. It is excellent biriyani and the AC might have kept it alive."

The bay was filled with the aroma of Punjabi delicacies. It stimulated my appetite. I looked at my hand and took out my lunch packet from the hook.

It was fresh. No damage. There was a white plastic spoon. It was chicken biriyani with a tempting smell. The lemon pickle kept in the small plastic pouch made me more contented.

I looked at Tina. Both she and Arjun were sharing one *thali* meal provided by the railway's pantry.

How the railway could ensure a uniform color of its daal, shape of the chappati and unique smell for years, I wondered. It's healthy food, but for patients, I felt, colorless, odorless and tasteless.

We Indians are colorful. Perhaps the railway wants us to be normal while travelling.

I felt happy to have a good dinner. Tomorrow morning, I will be with mom and I can get the food I like the best.

Something is compensated for me too. I felt less jealous of Tina, came down from my berth and gave company to my local guardian.

The Punjabi team looked tired. I sat nearer to Bindra uncle and smiled.

"Beta, you could sleep the entire day. If I sleep during the day, I have to sit counting down the whole night." He smiled and looked at me.

I liked Bindra uncle. He was frank.

"Uncle, I lost my sleep due to the exams and project work. I hope, I can sleep a couple of weeks; and at my home, I can compensate."

Suseela aunty adjusted my hair and asked,

"Are all the people in your village fair like you?"

The question embarrassed me. I looked at my hand and said,

"Aunty, I'm not fair like you." Keeping my hand next to hers, I said,

"Look, you are much fairer than me!"

Bindra uncle helped his wife, "Beta, she wants to check up whether you have any connection with Vasco Da Gama, so that she can have her next vacation in Portugal!"

He looked at Suseela aunty. She was not impressed by her husband's joke.

He added, "Her mission to Kanyakumari is to find any left-out ship of Vasco Da Gama and see whether she can row it back to his shore, keeping an eye on television cameras and finding a place in the Guinness Book!"

Pushpa aunty burst into laughter with Arora uncle. They could visualize Suseela aunty's rowing the old ship in her best chosen costume nearer to the beach and the television crew chasing her like the paparazzi after the late Princes Diana.

Suppressing his laughter, Arora uncle cracked,

"Do *Mallus* know that Vasco Da Gama first reached Punjab through the river and was attracted to see the long-haired villagers bathing and washing in river Ganga? The starved eyes of Vasco Da Gama and his crew rowed nearer to them. They were shocked to see beards on the village damsels, hurriedly rowed back to the sea, came nearer to Kozhikode, hit a rock and were forced to land there. Beta, Bindraji hails from the same village and it is known as Vasco *Bhagai*."

Arjun gestured hats off to Aroraji, shook his hand in admiration of the Punjabi skill in the molding of instantaneous stories and enjoyed the humor.

Bindraji was stunned. Perhaps for a moment he visualized being in the Ganga with his hair open at a young age and Vasco Da Gama with his crew getting scared on seeing the village women with beards.

Bindraji also hit Aroraji with his palms, and the bay was filled with energy and humor.

The train loved to run while cutting across the setting sun's red light.

I hoped that Bharathiya Rail should catch such moods on the camera, properly edit them and telecast them on popular television channels for building its brand. The railway is one of our finest instruments for national integration. It connects people, transports goods, animals, insects and even sustains a life system of its own. It also enables the penniless to travel. It has the longest connectivity through electric lines, communication networks and water supplies and even owns the longest open toilet. Each day, it accommodates a couple of millions: travellers, service providers, entertainers, vendors, pickpockets, thieves, beggars, criminals and so forth.

It has a unique culture of its own. It has its own smell. Its chai-pani, thali meals, sleeping kits, pantry services and so forth have unique features of their own. Nothing can match upto them. It empowers its travellers to be better tolerant through delays, cancellations, accidents and apathy. It is the largest of its kind in the world and attracts the smartest cabinet ministers.

It is the only mighty sector where students, daily commuters, elected representatives, women, defense personnel, senior citizens and the talented are acknowledged and accommodated. Every day, Bharathiya Rail enables more than 5 million passengers to commute and takes them to their respective destinations. A few millions spend a sizably long time in her. Often, they nap, sleep, meditate, recite *bhajans*, engage in petty talk and debates, discuss, shout, quarrel, push and pull and even dive into the rivers from them.

My Kerala Express made most of them sleep. She was making up for the next halt.

I looked out. A highway was running parallel to us. Headlights of the fast-running vehicles helped me see the large trucks loaded with containers. It may be a part of the Golden Quadrilateral connecting the national highways in the Indian subcontinent. Those movements reassured the fast economic growth of the great country.

I felt happy and looked at my co-passengers. All of them were happy, except Tina. Perhaps Arjun has to join his group, leaving her to the mercy of us, the Punjabi team, of which I'm a member.

The train dragged itself to the much-expected halt at Chittor.

He smiled, looked at the Punjabi members and said,

"Goodnight," and turning to Tina, he warned,

"You are to be here only. We shall meet you at Chengannur, tomorrow. The scheduled time is at 11:55 in the morning. You can have breakfast from the pantry boys."

He hurriedly left. He may have to run to reach his compartment. Perhaps those seniors have to travel in the second sleeper class in extreme summer due to the nonavailability of accommodation in the AC compartments and to be with Prof Bala during the hurriedly planned visit to Kerala.

Can't we plan our travel well in advance? I have to thank Kochamma. She booked our tickets from the railway reservation center at JNU. When I informed her of my viva date, on the first available date, she booked our tickets and the return ticket to Bhubaneswar for Tina on her request.

Travelling such long distances during extreme summer is really taxing. In the AC compartment with good food, it was relaxing and I can reach home fresh, I thought. The train pulled up. Tina's phone beeped and it assured her of the safety of Arjun and his team.

Like a robot, Tina said, "goodnight" and climbed to the top berth.

I looked at the Punjabi team. All were fast asleep. None of them slept during the day, except me. I felt comfortable and climbed to my berth.

The train picked up speed. Its filtered sound was friendly in the AC compartment. Within the last two days, we learned the art of living with Bharathiya Rail.

I could realize the comfort and limitation of the daily commuters and the service providers.

I also could realize why these groups love to talk about the train when they travel.

She may be caring for them, I felt. I too liked Kerala Express and found myself comfortable in her white sheet and small pillow.

Someone scratched me on my hand. I woke up on seeing Tina.

"It is 11:00 in the morning. We have passed Kottayam, Arjun says. Are we nearing Chenganoor?" Tina said.

I searched for my cell phone and checked the time. It was 11:20 in the morning. I struggled to get myself down from the sandwiched berth.

I managed to land myself on the floor and whispered to Tina,

"In less than half an hour we shall be at Chengannoor. We have to get ourselves decently dressed. Along with our parents, we have our own seniors in the train." I stared at Tina.

She rolled out and landed on the floor in her style.

For the first time, she obeyed me. Within ten minutes, we made ourselves in a presentable form. We shared our makeup sets and helped each other look presentable.

I chose a churidhar, and Tina preferred to have her newly purchased jeans and matching shirt that she had bought from Palika Bazaar.

Between the two elderly men, Bindra uncle, perhaps, might have been naughtier in his youth. Pretending to be deep in sleep, he was watching us and enjoying himself.

I approached him and in his ear, I made a noise resembling the low-pitched roar of a lion. He burst into laughter and got up from his berth.

Tina was unable to control her laugh. Enjoying the scene, Bindra uncle pleaded,

"Beta, can you mimic the giant's roar in Suseela's ears?"

With the most mischievous face, he added,

"Beta, be careful, she may jump out of the train, thinking that the local lions are chasing her for a Punjabi breakfast!"

I was scared. Bindra uncle and Tina encouraged me to do so.

To make them happy, I prompted half a dozen thunderous roars.

As expected, all the three woke up from their nap and stared at us. I pointed my finger to Bindraji and said,

"Aunty, Bindra uncle was imitating local cocks."

Aroraji climbed down from the top berth and said,

"Why don't you repeat it? That's quite funny, you attempted a cock-crow and it came out as Punjabi *Sher's* (lion) roaring!"

I gestured to Bindra uncle to fold his hands on his mouth and to act like he was mimicking a rooster. The moment he responded, I mimicked the jungle king's mighty roars and their challenge to impose authority.

The whole bay was filled with onlookers, and the Punjabi team became vibrant. Bindra uncle caught hold of me in Punjabi style and declared,

"Beta, I'm unable to accept that you'll be leaving us," and he looked at Suseela aunty.

She kissed my forehead and then Tina's and said,

"We enjoyed your company. Beta, all of you should visit us in Delhi. We are all aged, but when we spend time with you, we want to live longer," and she was on the verge of tears.

She looked at the onlookers, hurriedly collected her toiletries and went towards the toilet.

Aroraji helped us to collect and arrange our luggage on the upper berth. The train was half empty. We counted our bags to ensure they were there.

Pushpa aunty inquired, "How far is your home from the railway station?"

"Aunty, it is half an hour's drive. My parents will be there at the station."

Bindraji felt happy and said, "We all will be at the door and we want to wave to you, Arjun and your parents."

All the three agreed to the suggestions, and Bindraji looked for Suseela aunty.

The train slowed down. We picked up the luggage and went in the direction that Bindraji indicated, obviously for the convenience of Suseela aunty. We reached near the door and my phone beeped.

It was pappa. "Pappa, there are three boys in S7 and we have to drop them at Mangalam."

"All arrangements are made," he said.

There was a pause and he added,

"*Mole* (daughter), can you see us? We are on the platform."

The train reached the platform; it was nearing the halt, and my parents were nearer to us.

Bindraji gestured to us to be comfortable and he got down first. We too got down with our luggage.

I lifted up my mom's arm and waved at the aunties and Arora uncle.

By the time, Bindraji introduced himself to pappa and they were smiling. Bindraji embraced pappa in Punjabi style. A national integration process by the Bharathiya Rail, I felt.

By the time, Arjun and team approached us; they shook hands with pappa and Bindraji preferred the Punjabi style *galey lago* (embrace). Smilingly, he said *namasthe* to my mom and boarded the train.

They waved at us. I felt like parting from a group of the most loving and caring elders. True Indian culture is reflected in such moments. My moist eyes transcended the cultural ties, and the train moved slowly with vigorous hands waving from both sides.

⁂

We moved to the parking area. Pappa took one of the bags from Tina, held her elbow like a caring father with his mischievous child and walked in front of us.

I walked next to my mother and we reached the car, a white Innova. I was surprised to see Achachan and Ammama in the car.

This was the first time that both of them had come to receive me at the railway station. Perhaps, it was due to Bala uncle's guest.

But still, why had Achamma come? Something was in the air. The reason for the unusual reception baffled me.

Achachan came near, hugged me and kissed me on my forehead.

He wished all of us and stroked Tina's head. She touched his feet.

Achamma held me in her arms, turned me left and right to have a better look at me and said,

"My Chippy mol looks beautiful even after two days of tiresome journey. I was worried about how you would feel after the long journey."

Looking up at her favorite Sabarimala Sastha in the clouds, she chirped,

"It's all His will." She pulled me out from the group that was moving towards the Innova and said,

"Mole, we shall go in your pappa's car. Let the boys move to Mangalam with your Achachan. Bala has asked us to take care of them."

After the luggage was kept inside pappa's car, Tina and I walked towards Achachan and the group.

There was confusion among the boys. It was more visible on Arjun's face.

Achachan, with his towering figure, caught our attention and informed us,

"All the boys will join me and our Innova will go to Mangalam house. Chippy's dad will bring you to Mangalam for lunch before 2:00 in the afternoon. We can have lunch together."

He looked at me and smiled.

⁂

Achamma was holding my hand. I really wanted to talk to the boys. I felt dejected.

The Innova first moved out from the parking slot. Our Maruti followed. Achamma, Tina and I sat in the rear seat. Achamma was in the middle and was holding our wrists as if we were trying to escape.

I looked at Tina. She was getting uncomfortable and twisted her wrist. Achamma realized and slowly released her. But she gripped my wrist with added strength.

"Do you have any problem with Achachan?" I whispered. It struck her that she might have been holding us like prisoners. She released my wrist, smiled, lovingly gripped my thigh and said,

"When we reach home, you will get the rest of your punishment there," she whispered and once again held my wrist with her censored grip.

Mum looked at us now and then with her rationed teacher's smile. Maybe she is tied on duty with pappa to drive the car. When she sits with him, her body movements will match with those of the driver, my pappa. She doesn't know driving. But she always navigates pappa when he is at the wheel.

The Innova was not visible. They might have already reached Mangalam house, I thought.

In order to make us comfortable, Pappa asked,

"Tina, how were your exams?"

Tina's mind was ruminating on the green paddy fields in view. We covered part of Kuttanadu and were nearing our village. To wake Tina up from her dream, I leaned towards her and repeated papa's question,

"How were your exams? Pappa is asking."

"Oh! They were easy," she said and added,

"I'll be scoring high grades." She leaned forward and asked pappa,

"Uncle, do you find any changes in this place when compared with your school days?"

Pappa looked around and said,

"Yes, these roads, the culverts, the electric lines, moving vehicles and the bill boards are all new."

He paused and said,

"During my childhood, there were no concrete buildings. The paddy fields stretched till the coconut farms. In the midst of them, there were thatched houses. Small canoes carried men, women and children. Occasionally, large boats loaded with coconuts, coir, paddy straws and bamboo were rowed with the help of long bamboo poles. Fishermen, shell collectors and coir workers were seen more frequently."

He paused and added,

"We all used our own small canoes. It was after the 1970s that road transport developed. Today, people are more comfortable with bikes, autorickshaws and cars."

"Can you row a boat?" Tina asked me.

"Chippy can swim and row our canoes. I taught her," Achamma said.

"When you are at Mangalam, she will row you to see our relatives."

"We can reach most of the houses easily by canoes," pappa added.

"I can swim. But I never used a boat. In Bhubaneswar, we don't get an opportunity," Tina said.

❦❦❦

# 2

## At Onattukara

The car got onto National Highway 47 (NH 47), which leads to Alappuzha town. The tourism department's green board indicated twenty-eight kilometers to the town. Our Maruti gained speed under the watchful eyes of the pilot.

The compound gate was kept open, and Manikutty came running towards the car. I call her Mani *Akka* (elder sister). She was around forty years of age, was well built and had a pleasant face. Her younger son studied in the nearby school where my mom was working as a teacher. Her elder son was studying in the sports school at Patiala. The old Rajdooth motorbike of Mani Akka's husband, Ajith Kumar, was parked near the gate. It meant that he was at home. He was an attender in the nearby Primary Agriculture Credit Society. I called him Ajith Chettan. He was better known in the village as "agent." He dealt with land, animals and anything saleable. Often, he also worked as a marriage broker. The agent made three times more money doing this than the salary he received from the society and built a beautiful house for Mani Akka. The husband and wife spent a larger part of their day in Mangalam house along with my grandparents. Based on their needs, they also helped my parents.

We stepped inside the house. It was neat and tidy. In my room, two beds were arranged and Tina sat on the one by the side of the window. I sat on the other bed and was planning to lie down, when Achamma came in and said,

"Why don't you take a bath and dress up nicely?"

I looked at what she had brought and kept on my bed: a white pearl necklace, matching *jimica* (hanging earrings) along with the traditional costume of Kerala, mundu and neriyathu.

"Why, am I going to perform Mohiniattom in Mangalam?" I said, mimicking its popular movements.

Achamma tried hard to hide her smile. Instead, her tone was firm when she said,

"It is an important occasion in your life. So just do as I say and get dressed quickly."

She placed the white pearl necklace around my neck and asked me to hold the eardrops against my ears.

Tina took the eardrops from the bed, held them against her ears and positioned herself before the mirror.

It looked good on her, I thought.

Now mum came in with a bottle of our homemade shampoo.

"Here is shampoo for you girls," she said, giving Tina a mundu and neriyathu set.

"You can also try our mundu and neriyathu."

Tina looked at the mundu-neriyathu set with a red border; she was in a fix.

"Aunty, I don't have a matching blouse with me," she said.

"Don't worry, I will get you a matching blouse and skirt," mum said and she added, "You can wear these for Arjun."

Tina, who was lying flat on her bed, sat up on hearing this and she looked a little embarrassed.

In a flash, she took the shampoo, her towel and went inside the bathroom.

Achamma, amused by Tina's escape, said,

"You have to be your best in appearance. During the entire week, we shall celebrate at Mangalam house with guests and our family members." She gestured me to go nearer; I sat in front of her chair on the floor and put my head in her lap. And, I cracked,

"Your majesty, the Queen of Mangalam and the most beautiful wife of Achachan, your granddaughter will obey your orders!"

I looked at her and again hid my face in her lap. She held me and beat me softly on my back.

But she looked deep in thought. Her body was warm and I could feel the warmth of her love.

Mom returned with the blouses and underskirts for Tina and me.

"Who will help her to wear mundu and neriyathu?" I wondered,

"Don't worry. Someone will help her. I have already told the girls in the neighborhood,"

Mum said without looking at me.

Assuming the position of the regular teacher that she was, she added,

"look, you wash your hair. I'll help you to have a *Kulipinnal* (a traditional Kerala hair arrangement). After lunch, you can change to your convenience." She pulled out my head from Achamma's lap.

"You are no more a child. You are twenty-three. By that age, you were in my belly."

"That's not your merit. It was due to the smartness of Achamma's son, Adv. Babu," I shouted. Achamma hit me hard on my back and said,

"Look Laila, JNU could change your daughter. It's heard that the majority of them are terrorists and she might have chosen one among them."

She hit me on my back again and said,

"Go and take your bath," and she left the room.

I looked at the dress and ornaments. I felt the absence of my terrorist. God alone knows what he is at, in Mussoorie?

Tina is lucky. The rat will shine in Mangalam! What is the family function that these people are talking about?

I took my dress, ornaments and the cane kit holding the shampoo and went inside pappa's toilet. It was well kept. Mom was good at it.

I was happy on seeing myself in my traditional attire. I put sandal paste on my forehead with a little kumkum at its center.

For the *Kulipinnal*, I searched for mum. There was a lot of noise on the veranda. A small crowd was helping Tina to wear the traditional dress. Mum was the leader.

I went back to pappa's room, tied my hair in the form of the Kerala *Kulipinnal* and kept a small piece of tulsi leaf in the knot. I searched for the sandalwood oil, as mom used to always hide the bottle in her dressing table. I could locate it and use it profusely. I also wanted to search her cupboard. But it was not timely and so, I postponed the same to a working day, when she would be at her school.

Near the gate, I saw a few men standing in a group and pappa was also with them. I ran towards the gate. I saw an electrician clinging on the top of an electric pole and connecting wires. Pappa looked at his watch and said,

"It's time, we should move to Mangalam." By this time, Tina and the others also joined us.

"During the week, both of you can stay at Mangalam and join the study team. Based on the request of the Delhi team, your Achachan has just informed me about the requirement. Therefore, you may collect necessary items for your stay at Mangalam upto Thursday." Saying this, pappa walked into the house and called out, "Amma, Lalila, please come out."

Turning to Ajith, he said in a very low voice,

"You lock the house and both of you join us at Mangalam."

Tina was happy. She ran to the room and hurriedly brought her bags. I too followed her, cursing my fate.

Pappa ignited his car. It was his usual practice to flush out mum and team from the house.

We loaded the bags in the boot. I took the front seat along with papa and smiled at him. Rarely does he allow such intrusion.

The car slowly moved out from the portico, and its hoverings made the two ladies rush towards it. Poor Tina was sandwiched, and she looked like a bride who was hesitant to marry an elderly groom.

I enjoyed her helplessness.

The car moved at an unusual speed. Adv. Babu is smarter today, I felt.

Achamma tried to arrange my hair and whispered,

"I asked the agent to bring fresh pichipoove (jasmine flowers) from the market. All of us should wear it." And she continued to arrange my hair. It was only 1:40 in the afternoon. Pappa was looking at his watch and driving fast.

We reached Mangalam house and were surprised to hear,

"Happy Birthday Achamma!!"

Mani Akka's second son was the leader of a group with half a dozen neighboring boys and girls.

Achamma was quite shy and she never expected such a show, especially in the presence of the Delhi group. She looked at her husband and Ajith and complained to Manikutty,

"At least you could have given me a hint so that I could have visited the temple."

"It's all planned by Achen and Aji chettan. They wanted to give you a surprise and Achen didn't want anyone of us in the kitchen today. So, the food arrangement is done by Aji Chettan's friends."

"Chippy, *kattan kapi* (black coffee), your favorite."

Mani Akka woke me up. She brought two mugs: One was empty, and the other was full with Mangalam special coffee that was made from freshly ground coffee beans that were mixed with pepper, ginger and jaggery. Its aroma filled the room.

"I have made tea for the guest."

Looking at Tina, who was still sleeping, she said,

"If she likes coffee, you can share with her. For the boys, I have kept the tea tray and a coffee jug on the veranda. You may serve them." She smiled and walked out of the room.

"I too want coffee."

Tina jumped out of her bed, caught Mani Akka and dragged her into the room.

Mani Akka never expected it. She wriggled and said,

"This girl needs to be married immediately."

She came out of her grip and commented,

"I will tell Achamma about the urgency to get her married."

Saying this, she ran away from the room.

"What did she say? I didn't get her."

Tina fell into her own trap early in the morning. Looking at me, she wanted an answer.

Suddenly, Mani Akka reemerged with a mug full of coffee for Tina. Handing over the mug to her, she whispered,

"This girl will never allow that poor boy to sleep. I have kept all the items on the table. Your boy may also like Mangalam coffee. Go and enjoy the coffee with him." She turned to go.

Tina took a sip of the coffee. She turned her face towards Mani Akka and said,

"Oh! This is amazing. You are an expert in making coffee." She put the coffee mug on the table, ran to Akka and planted a quick kiss on her cheek.

Mani Akka blushed, and she pretended to run away from the room.

"Why don't you serve the coffee to the boys?" she reminded.

"Yes, I will. But don't you want to see Arjun!" I teased.

Taking our mugs, we followed Mani Akka and we were surprised to see Achachan with Arjun, Praful and Alex already enjoying the coffee.

"Good morning, we were waiting for you to talk about today's program," Achachan announced.

There was a bit of a silence

Praful went nearer to Achachan and said,

"Sir, we came here, because of Prof Saxena, a close friend of Prof Bala, who would guide us in carrying out a research project to trace out certain missing links in our history. We feel that a detailed study of the history of the local areas and the people will throw light on the subject. They advised us to seek your help in planning the study at Onattukara as a part of our project."

"Today is Monday. We have only four days left. On Friday, Bala and family will reach here and we all will be busy with them. However, till Thursday, I will be with you as a local guide," Achachan added.

"I'm ninety-one. I was born and brought up in Onattukara. I had seen, listened, observed and read a few things about this area. I shall be glad to share my views with your team. I will also take you to a few important places around the said Sree Moolavasam, the Holy Buddhist seat of learning that was submerged under the sea, centuries ago."

"Prof Bala had given us a brief sketch of Arattupuzha Velayudha Panicker (AVP)," Praful intervened. Looking at Achachan, he continued,

"You being one of the close relatives of AVP, we seek your guidance to collect information on the *thuruth* (island) where AVP lived. We would like to visit his ancestral home, the temple established by him and study the geographical settings of the island." He paused and looked at Alex to supplement what he was saying.

"Under the project, not less than ten such important pockets will be selected from the west coast during the first phase of the study. Another team will cover the east coast and will identify important pockets for similar studies." Alex paused and added,

"The attempt is to document the missing links, often known as the Dark Age of India. So it's a long-driven teamwork. And, we hope, a few research agencies and their scholars will participate in exploring our own rich past, a great period in which we have less evidence, more stories and myth," Alex continued,

"We will also attempt visual documentation of the historical sites in Onattukara. This will enable us to draw preliminary inferences on geography, culture and socioeconomic settings of the local area."

Arjun intervened and asked,

"Can we also join you?"

"Eight people can travel in an Innova," Achachan said. Looking at the group he had a quick head count and said, "All of you can join. We are only seven."

He looked at Arjun and Tina and said,

"These kids will be comfortable in the rear seat."

With his own peculiar mischievous eyes, he looked at the others and all laughed. Tina felt elated and expressed the same to me through a nice pinch. Cursing my fate, I remembered Neeraj.

Praful moved and stood before the large oil painting of AVP that adorned the wall.

"Why does AVP have a peculiar hair dressing?" he asked.

"He lived between 1825 and 1874. It was the time of hair knots for gents. Cutting the knot was a violation of the social law in certain pockets. Knots were tied either on the back of the head or on the top of the head and were placed on left and right sides of the head to show the identity and even caste of a person. Violators were punished in the mainland. Thus, AVP might have adopted his own hair style. In Arattupuzha and especially in Mangalam, the knot was not compulsory. Only those who moved to the mainland followed the discipline."

Achachan went nearer to the painting and pointed,

"Even the newly introduced police in Travancore had a different haircut. This may be an improvised style of the Travancore Raja (southern part of the current Kerala state) Marthanda Varma or Rama Varma (1847–80) and the British representative in Travancore, Colonel Munroe."

Alex was closely observing the painting, and he murmered,

"He seems to be rich, as reflected in his dressing and ornaments. Look at his golden studs and pearl mala."

"Yes, you are right. His forefathers were successful merchants during the seventeenth and eighteenth centuries. They had trade relations with Arab and Kutch traders, who used to go to the thuruth to buy copra, coir, dry fish and arrack. Before King

Marthanda Varma's annexation of the Nadus (small provinces), they were ruled by Naduvazhikal (chieftains). In the thuruth, AVP's family took the responsibility of tending to the local leaders. As the approach to the thuruth was only through boats, the chieftains of the neighboring areas didn't dare to cross the water." Saying this, he paused.

"How large is the thuruth?" Alex enquired.

"The thuruth is currently eleven kilometers in length and three kilometers in width. In certain places, the width is as narrow as fifty meters. On one side is the Arabian Sea and on the other side is Sasthamkotta kayal (lake). Currently, about 800 families live here. Sea erosion has consumed one-fourth of the earlier available land. A good number of our coconut plantations were lost during the past seventy-five years." He paused and added,

"Being one of the great-grandsons of AVP, I inherited seventeen acres of coconut plantation, which I had shared with my two sons. I remember my grandfather telling me that Panickarachan, AVP had inherited more than 300 purayidam (plots of land) from his grandfather. We heard that during his time he had 18,000 coconut-yielding plants and he cultivated paddy in more than 400 acres."

Interrupting Achachan, Praful asked,

"Will you please explain to us the living conditions in Arattupuzha during your childhood?"

Achachan had drawn one of the cane chairs and sat in front of the oil canvas of AVP. Looking at the painting, he closed his eyes and tried to recapture his memory.

"My great-grandmother was AVP's daughter. So, I belong to the fourth generation. I'm ninety-one and can recollect certain features of the thuruth eighty years earlier." Then, he paused.

"I also heard from elders stories on Arattupuzha and its neighborhood, popularly known as Onattukara, the current Karthikapally, Karunagapally, Mavelikara and Kayamkulam area. Elders generally do not misguide their sons and grandsons. So you can depend on me for certain clues pertaining to

Onattukara. Your area of interest may be to explore a 1,000-year history of India, to dwell more on Sreemoolavasam here and our heroes like AVP. But to trace the social history, you have to start at least from the time of Mahabali, the beloved Pallava king loved by the people of Onattukara. The culture that Mahabali nursed still prevails in this area."

"Malayalis celebrate Onam, a post harvest festival, and recreate their lost culture and celebrate it for ten days," Praful added.

"No, the culture is never lost and such a rich heritage can never be lost." Achachan was firm in his voice.

"The inherited rich culture still prevails, and I've seen it with my own eyes, in terms of such colorful cultural activities in Onattukara among her people. If you are serious in your research, you can find the great culture in our thuruth and its adjacent places even today."

Achachan appeared nostalgic. He focused on the painting and added in a low voice,

"From the river side, daily bullock carts moved along with labor who came from Kizhakkekara (eastern side of the river) to work in the coconut farms and paddy fields. During my childhood, in certain places, the sea was at a distance of five to six kilometers from the river side, and we took twenty to thirty minutes to reach the beach by bullock cart. During such routine trips, from elders, we heard that the sea was eight to ten kilometers further away. During such trips, they sang songs and narrated stories to pass the time."

Achachan looked pleasant. He gazed on each one of us and continued,

"Our houses were near the river side. We had two dogs, Veeru and Pandu. Veeru was fond of me and followed our cart when I was with the elders. We had food arrangements near the sea in a thatched shed. Veeru used to enjoy the food and loved to sleep in the shadows nearer to the beach side. Before the sun set, we used to return to our homes after the day's work."

"How was the land stretching upto the sea?" Praful was serious and took notes in his diary.

"On both sides of the village lane, there were large plots that had coconut, plantain, vegetables and sesame. In certain farms, boundaries were made with the locally available shrub, known as *kalli*. For the purpose of fencing, dried stems of kalli and coconut palm leaves were used. There were a few hundred similar farms with mixed cropping patterns. Along with us, a few families also carried out the farm operations. After 1950, many families preferred to move to the mainland, especially nearer to the National Highway (NH 47). By that time, road transport also developed. After Indian independence, our family moved to Nangiyarkulangara junction, which was by the side of the highway."

Drawing the cane chair nearer to Achachan, Praful enquired,

"Have you noticed any processing and trading activities in the thuruth during your childhood?"

Achachan got the hint and explained,

"In my memory, copra and fish drying continued. Very rarely, I saw coir making. Only a few families retted the coconut cover and made fiber. Paddy processing was not observed. When the connecting bridge was made during the early 1950s, trucks came and collected the agricultural produce. Trading mostly took place in Alappuzha market or in the emerging market at Karunagapally. Resettlement of the entrepreneurs to the new areas, especially in Alappuzha town and the surrounding area of Karunagapally market, reduced the importance of Arattupuzha and our thuruth."

Mani Akka emerged with Achamma.

"Breakfast is ready," she said.

Achamma gave the routine *pachilamarunnu* (herbal medicine) to Achachan along with water filled in a copper vessel.

Turning to me, she said,

"All of you, get ready. Ajith mon will be back soon. He has gone to the market to buy fish and vegetables."

We met at the dining table around 8:30 in the morning, and Mani Akka had supplemented Kerala Perotta with *Vella Appam* (a traditional Kerala delicacy made of fermented rice powder, coconut milk, sugar and yeast or toddy for fermentation) and egg masala. The group almost finished the Appam, and Praful said,

"I will try Kerala parotta," helping himself to one.

Achamma understood Praful's courtesy and said,

"Don't worry, you have parotta and mixed-vegetable curry for lunch. Achachan will return around 1:30 in the afternoon. You can have lunch in the canteen near Mangalam Temple and move around till evening."

Mani Akka placed two polythene bags in front of Tina and showed her the lunch packets and water bottles.

# 3

## Kallassery Tharavad and Mangalam Temple

At 10:30 in the morning, we approached Mangalam village. During the twelve minute drive from Nangyarkulangara to Mangalam, Tina was holding her breath, looking at both sides of the road. There was even no whisper from the rear seat, though she was with Arjun. They were lost at the sight of the rivulets cutting across the length and breadth of Arattupuzha. On both sides of the road, a variety of activities was going on. Moving canoes were filled with paddy straw, coir fiber, coconuts, timber, firewood and construction materials; students and ladies were hurrying to schools and markets.

When the car took a turn towards Mangalam village, the sea waves and the wind welcomed us with a spray of sea water. Our lips tasted salty. The naughty sea breeze chased our car, often adding to its speed.

Tina was unable to control herself. Forgetting Achachan's presence in the car, she said,

"Chippy, shall we run along the beach?"

Achachan has sharp ears. He said,

"In the evening, you can walk and run along the eight-kilometer stretch. Ajith will be with you and you need not have any fear while moving and talking to any person in the thuruth."

The car approached a narrow strip, where the sea and the river almost met.

Both the mighty sea and the mischievous river licked the tender tip of the land.

It was unique.

"The land is fragile," Praful said, sharing his concern.

"Will this not result in the mixing of the water from both the sides during the monsoon?" he asked.

Achachan could read Praful's mind.

"Occasionally, it happens. During severe monsoon, we had such incidents and we had knee-deep water in the island. We are island dwellers and could read the conduct of both the sea and the river. When there is a threat, we move to safer places and small boats are always kept ready for meeting such emergencies. All of us know swimming and life in the thuruth has its own unique features. There is a belief that nature will not be hostile and a divine spirit is always there to take care of us."

He paused, looked at Praful and added,

"There is an unbelievable binding among the people here. They quarrel and fight as usual. But they seldom violate the local practices and customs. They love their land in between the two waters. For the people in the thuruth, if the river is their mother, the mighty sea is their father, which is contrary to the general concept of *Kadalamma* for the fishermen living on the coastal side. Can you believe that even a child in this thuruth will not piss in sea water? The dependence on both the waters is a great culture and it continues."

The car was moving at a low speed. Ajith, who had been Achachan's close companion for the past two decades, knows how to interpret his signals as well. To Achamma, he is Ajith mon (sweet son), especially when her own sons are not around. She feels that her husband who has crossed ninety years is safe when Ajith mon is around. Her confidence in him and his wife Manikutty makes her happy and her house vibrant.

"Sir, was this street present during your childhood?" Alex asked.

It was easy for Achachan to look at Alex, who was sandwiched between Praful and me. The space in the Innova allowed him to turn to Alex.

"This road got its importance only after the completion of the two connecting bridges we had just seen. Otherwise, it was just a path only. The sea was not around. It was atleast two kilometers away. During our childhood, we could never see the sea while walking along the path or moving in a cart. The coconut palms and other vegetative cover never allowed us to see more than 100 meters. The whole area was thickly vegetated. The coconut farms were dense. Each tree yielded on an average thirty to forty nuts at every forty-day interval. The less yielding trees were used for toddy tapping. The movements of the toddy tappers and coconut-yielding teams were frequent. The female participation in fish drying, coconut palm leaf mending, preparation of fire wood, maintenance of the milch animals, rearing of backyard poultry and ducks, washing clothes, and maintenance of the house and its surroundings made this area appear busy during the day."

He continued,

"The bridges helped enhance better road connectivity through bullock carts and of late, through cars and trucks. In the first stage, the road was made with gravel that was brought from the mainland. It happened during the 1960s only. Within another decade, it was changed to a blue metal road, and by the 1980s, we had a tarred road. Availability of the blue metal roads encouraged private bus owners to start bus services upto Thrikkunnapuzha Temple, which you have seen at the entry point. Then, it was extended to Mangalam and later upto the southern tip of the *thuruth*. Of late, a new bridge is also available for public use. The bridge is wide, and people at Mangalam prefer to pass through the new bridge to reach NH 47."

***

Our car took a left turn from the road and parked near the temple compound. It was fifty meters away from the main road. The side road went around the temple compound. At the eastern side of the compound, Edakkal Government Higher Secondary School was seen. The AVP Memorial Auditorium, Edakkal Gnaneswara Kshethram Yogam Office, Arattupuzha Grama Panchayat's Government L. P. School, Shri G. Divakaran

Memorial Auditorium, the age-old temple, its *Pattambalam* (prayer hall) and the Lotus Pond were visible from the area at which we had assembled.

Achachan wanted to meet the office bearers of the temple and as he was leaving us, he said,

"You move around the temple and the remains of the Nalukettu, the ancestral house of AVP. Chippy will explain the details to you. I will have a chat with the temple administrators and wait for you."

We were all enthusiastic on seeing AVP's house, the Nalukettu. Kerala Nalukettu consists of a rectangular structure with a courtyard at the center, four rooms and four corner rooms. The courtyard has four corridors that are in the shape of swastika.

A portion of the Nalukettu stood there, challenging time. It bared a metal tag of the local panchayat, indicating house No. 183 and Ward No. XVII. It had a tiled roof. The tiles carried the imprint, Devi Tiles, Quilon Tiles and Ashtamudi Tiles. The structure of the roof and side walls was made of wood. Long years of wind from both the river and the sea made wrinkles on them. Each piece of wood called out, "I'm 150 years plus." One part of the floor was tiled and the other part was cemented, probably reflecting the maintenance carried out over 150 years.

The remaining portion was facing the east, and its front elevation had a *pathayam* (bed-cum storage) with side- and top-opening doors. Next to it was a seating arrangement for visitors. This portion of the Nalukettu might have been used by AVP 130 years ago for building a partnership with the people of the thuruth with *Karuna* (compassion), *Mudita* (happiness at the welfare of others) and *Maithri* (universal love).

The whole house and compound reflected emptiness. We all felt like deaf and dumb for a while, and we heard nothing except the feeble footsteps and the sounds of the sea. Not even the sound of a crow broke the tranquillity. The whole place looked like a storyteller waiting for his or her listeners to assemble.

Arjun held Tina's hand and slowly walked around the remains. They appeared sad and scared. Tina's lips were pale and she followed Arjun in silence like a scared child.

Alex sat at a corner and filled in his notepad with notes and sketches. He looked lost. The occasional sound of the waves reminded us of the presence of the mighty Arabian Sea around.

Praful climbed on to the side wall near the arch and used his handkerchief to rub and observe certain writing on the wood on the ceilings. He whispered certain things to Alex and he took down the details in his notepad. These brilliant researchers of Delhi University were on their serious investigations.

I stood aloof in a corner. I've seen the ruins ample number of times; they looked one and the same and made me sad.

I moved out and sat on a piece of the ruin under a shade. The sea breeze carried tiny water particles, which entered through my cotton churidhar and tickled my skin. I remembered my "terrorist." If he were around, I could have explained to him all I know about this *Tharavad* (family).

But this group is on a larger expedition. They are unearthing a 1,000-year-old untold history. I'll ask my brother to invent a small machine in which I can sit holding my naughty terrorist and ski down to the millennium to see what exactly happened and how vested interests destroyed the rich past. My machine should be able to videograph, and we can show it to the public at Ram Leela Ground in Delhi. I enjoyed daydreaming about such fantasies. The wind swept my hair all over my face and it got all unruly.

"You should tie your hair," Ajith Chettan shouted. I woke up from my dream to see him standing with a rarely seen face.

"This area is like a temple. You are no more a child. People will be observing you. We've to safely hand you over to a prospective district collector," he said, continuing his sermon.

I stood up and tied my hair in seconds. He smiled and said,

"Still like a child. Come on, we will go to the office. Let them move around."

I felt irritated and shouted at him,

"What're you saying fala-fala? I'll tell Mani Akka that you have scolded me."

He was afraid of Mani Akka, I knew. Before her, all his smartness will vanish. I have even seen her smelling his mouth when he is around Bala uncle and his local friends with the bottles brought from duty-free shops. When he came to the kitchen for collecting the munchies, especially the duck fry, Bala uncle's favorite, Mani Akka used her own alcohol-smelling detector.

"You tell her a thousand times. She's more responsible. I'm just a *varuthan* (outsider) in Mangalam." He appeared serious and I walked just like a child behind him.

***

People around Achachan are extra sentimental, I felt. Hurting them is a risk that I would rather avoid.

A small array of tender coconuts with straws waited for the research team.

The secretary of the temple had kept aside a few old files and records for the perusal of the research team.

It was getting hot and humid. The sun in Arattupuzha reminded us of the mid-May heat in Delhi. The ceiling fan and the sea breeze gave some relief. Drawing a chair right under the ceiling fan, I glanced through the old records.

When Praful and the team reached, Achachan requested the secretary to share the information based on their interest.

Praful was a thorough professional. Even for a pilot study, he loved to hear from the right people.

After the introduction, Praful said,

"Secretary sahab, we are interested in collecting the information on AVP, his ancestral home, its neighborhood, the temple he established and the local feel and spirit of the people."

He paused and kept his scribbling pad ready. Alex assisted Praful, his senior, with his camera.

Ajith Chettan served the tender coconuts to all of us. With a silent node from Achachan, the secretary said,

"I'm a soldier and served in the Indian Army for twenty-nine years. For the past one decade, I am associated with the temple in various capacities. We've formed a *samithi(committee)* and our *vakil* (advocate) is the president. We have certain records available in this office and I"ve kept them for you."

He paused and shoved the records towards Praful.

"We've seen the remains of Kallassery Tharavadu, where AVP was born in 1825. The remains were part of a rich Nalukettu. The southern part, or locally known as *thekkeni,* which was meant for the male members is intact. We are interested in knowing more details about the *tharavadu,* the ancestoral house."

Praful focused on his requirements.

The secretary looked at Achachan and said,

"From the records available at this temple, it is understood that Perumal Achan (AVP's grandfather) had built the Nalukettu approximately twenty to thirty years before AVP's birth. Therefore, the house is definitely around 200 years old. From the structure, it may be seen that earlier it had a thatched roof, which was later converted into tiles. Three set of tiles manufactured by Quilon Tiles, Devi Tiles and Ashtamudi Tiles are seen on the roof. These factories have less than a 150-year history. Earlier, the house had a sprawling campus, more than five acres with gardens, cattle sheds, store houses and an outhouse for visitors and associates. Perumal Achan could afford them, because he was one of the successful traders who had his own mercantile vessels and support systems to produce bulk quantities of farm produce such as coconut, paddy, plantain and so forth on his own farms that stretched for more than 1,000 acres of land within the thuruth itself. He also encouraged fishermen to capture marine and fresh waterfish. They salted and dried them and sold bulk quantities to the traders, especially those arriving from the Kutch region in Gujarat and those from Arab countries. This created wealth. He might have deployed the surplus in his business and a part of it may have been used for the welfare of the people in the thuruth. It is said that the Nalukettu was made perfectly based on ancient Thatchu and Vasthu Sasthra. He paused.

"If it was built more than 200 years earlier based on Vasthu Sasthra, how come AVP died at a young age while living there?" Alex raised his doubt.

"We have regular visitors here and a few of the experts commented on the merits of the location of the house. Due to the north-west location of the Nalukettu and its east-facing location, it is said that the structure will survive for more than a millennium, which appears strange to us. It has already sustained 200 years. It may survive, perhaps to tell its own stories to the future generations."

He paused and again looked at Achachan, who nodded to go ahead.

"Subsequent construction of the temple might have perhaps brought calamity to its occupants. As per Vastu, a house on the right side of a Siva Temple will cause calamity to its occupants. But careful nurture of the same will bring unimaginable prosperity, name and fame to its inhabitants and owners." The secretary looked at Alex to see his reaction.

"Do you believe in such things even during the twenty-first century?" Alex probed.

"It is not our belief and faith. It's our experience that he has shared. In the past eighty years, I've been observing that it has become difficult to live in that house. Anyone even thinking of renovating or readdressing the values of the structure experiences financial prosperity but is still unhappy. A feeling of incomplete duties haunts them. Look at the structure. It has been standing there as a question mark for more than 200 years right in between the sea and the river, bearing torrential rains, gushy winds and the summer heat. It represents a great survival."

Looking at the secretary, Achachan said, "Sorry for the interruption, you may continue."

The room was filled with fresh nostalgia. The secretary continued,

"The people at Mangalam still call it *Kallasserypura* (Kallassery house), and the land around the Nalukettu is called *Kallassery Purayidom* (Kallassery plot). The *pura* (house) was accessible by all the people in Arattupuzha, especially those in Mangalam village. There were no formalities followed in their approach. Even today, all the *Karakkar* (local people) feel equally important. The subdivision of land by the family members made Kallassery Purayidom a smaller landholding, which is now less than three acres. It is currently not generating an income. So, similar to an age-old tusker left alone in the deep forest, the *tharavadu* waits for timely changes to happen."

Alex was perusing the records kept on the table. He flagged a few and discussed them with Praful.

"Secretary *sahab*, do you have any records about AVP's childhood?" Praful asked.

"There are a couple of booklets, research articles and press coverage on AVP. We have collected and preserved them. Based on such information, AVP was born in 1825 in Kallassery *tharavadu*. His mother was Perumal Achan's eldest daughter. His father, Govinda Panicker, hailed from Eruva, a village in Kayamkulam, which was a princely province thirty kilometers away from the *thuruth*. His mother died when he was only thirteen days old. He was brought up by Perumal Achan, his grandfather. We don't have much information on his father, Govinda Panicker, who died when AVP was a child. So, he was influenced by his grandfather, a successful farmer-cum-merchant. When he was sixteen years of age, his grandfather also died and he had to take leadership in Kallassery *tharavadu* as *karanavar*. The concept of *tharavadu* appears to be that of an important institution. The *karanavar* of the *tharavadu* had a lot of powers. This enabled the *tharavad* to update their knowledge and skills and to build relations with people engaged in production, trade and transport. The process enabled them to generate wealth. Alummoottil, Varanapally, Puthenthara, Coparathu, Kottoor, Variyath and so forth were a few *tharavadu* in earlier Odanadu."

He paused and showed us an album containing a few drawings of AVP, the Nalukettu and the local area.

Looking at them Arjun commented,

"He appears to be tall, well built and handsome."

"Yes, he was more than six feet tall and had an athletic body. He was an expert in *Kalari* (martial art) and wrestling. During his adolescent stage, large wrestling matches and Kalari practices were organized in the *thuruth* by Perumal Achan in response to his loving grandson's request. He loved AVP and taught him Malayalam, Sanskrit and Tamil with the help of local *Asan* (teachers). It is said that AVP also excelled in swimming." The secretary paused and looked at Achachan.

"During my childhood, in three different places, Kalari Asans, Gymnasia, *Ezhuthassans* (teachers helping one to learn reading and writing) and *Pallikkoodams* (schools) were active in the *thuruth*. Ezhuthassans and Kalari Assans used to come from different places and stayed in the *thuruth* to teach the local students. Both boys and girls came to the Pallikkoodam. But Kalari was made available only for boys. For girls also, in certain rich houses, arrangements were made for their training. I remember a couple of lady Kalari teachers who taught girls various exercises for flexibility of their bodies and also how to use small weapons for self-defense."

Achachan appeared to be immersed in his childhood memories. Tina and Arjun were lost in Achachan's childhood times. Almost like children, they heard and moved with Achachan in the Kalari and Asan's schools.

"The tradition of Asan's schools and *Gurukulams* for higher learning prevailed in the thuruth till the 1960s. Only after the regularization of the current modern school culture, the tradition became extinct. Perhaps, during the past millennium, these *Asans* and *Gurus* kept the vast majority of the Indians literate with the aid of a strong and well-spread institutional arrangement in each Indian village. The subject is worthy for conducting in-depth research. Otherwise, how could a few

Avarnas retain the vital arts, namely reading, writing, creative thinking and contribution to the subcontinent, even during the long stretch of the Dark Age?"

Achachan sought reactions from the research team.

Alex moved nearer to the secretary and enquired,

"Do we have any Asan Pallikkoodom in the thuruth?"

"No, now nursery schools, tuition and coaching centers are here.

A few of them are run by school teachers. Of late, coaching centers imparting training for medical and engineering entrance examinations have started dominating the show. Our temple administration also looks into the possibility of generating supplementary income by constructing new buildings to meet its increasing demand on rent."

Praful smiled and said,

"Alex, it's not the time of AVP. Now money matters and the thuruth also may be facing the influx of investors both from within and from the mainland. It's globalization, liberalization and competition."

All of us laughed.

"We too were champions in the globalization process," Achachan added.

"In Arattupuzha, we had direct trade with foreign traders during the last few centuries. Historically, it was a vibrant trade center when the adjoining Purakkad and the earlier Sreemoolavasam were flourishing at different periods. Perhaps, during that time, globalization happened in terms of trade and commerce was much more vibrant. That may be the reason for the tiresome expeditions from the west; Vasco Da Gama made it after 300 years of the state-supported voyages. I feel our forefathers had more variety of life. Different people, various types of food, plants, animals and gifts that were both brought and exchanged. Each day in the *thuruth* and similar areas in the coastal belt, life was vibrant, beautiful and a celebration."

Achachan paused, looked at Praful with his sparkling eyes and said,

"All of you should move into the village during afternoon hours and observe the local activities. The entire thuruth will look like a single house celebrating a marriage the next day. The activities are transparent among the houses. If someone is happy or unhappy, it is known to all. And people help each other, even today. There are no barriers based on income, caste and creed. In the thuruth, we don't have different faiths. All are like the leftover. No religious conversion took place here. Maybe there was less scope for that to happen. People are engaged in their work, and they are happy. The temple might have added to meeting the timely required demand of the people for socioeconomic and spiritual reasons. In earlier days, a local economy developed around a *Pally* (a place where people assembled to listen to the teachers) and later, a temple/church/mosque or market. The culture of the people here should be closely studied. It is local and reflects the rich Indian tradition. With your collective effort, I'm sure you will unveil many interesting insights related to our real tradition. All religions, customs, systems and practices have heavily drawn from the rich past. In the thuruth, you may perhaps observe these in their original form without much mixing. Due to the cutoff geographical condition, the strong internal administration or the small size of the area, it could retain, to a large extent, the original tradition. You can perhaps consider it a controlled sample to know about the Dark Age of India."

Looking at Praful, Achachan added,

"Praful, we don't have any specific religion in the thuruth. Even the influence of Christianity and Islam in the mainland is missing here. We are sitting near the Siva Temple that AVP had built for his loving people, maybe due to their constant demands. But I doubt whether the people are Hindus! It's a subject worthy for research. Their faith even today depends more on love and compassion and not on revenge."

"It looks strange to me," Praful said.

"You call me Achachan! Why? Because Chippy calls me that name and you simply did the same for the past two days, as you probably felt it was convenient to do so during your brief mission for a week. Isn't it so?"Achachan looked for an answer from Praful and Alex.

"Yes, it is. We love to call you Achachan without knowing its in-depth meaning," Alex said.

"Yes, that's my point." Achachan pulled them to his side and said,

"For some reason, we called these people Hindus. But they aren't. They are the "Leftover" Buddhists in India. Many of them are still sticking to the mighty culture that they had acquired between 500 BC and 1200 AD. Large changes have taken place in India after 1200 AD. For convenience, during those periods, the minority and those in power called these people by many names. In Kerala, those who captured power stamped the majority as Avarnas. It is the British who restamped them as "Hindus," a term used earlier by Max Muller to denote the people living in the subcontinent. Unfortunately, under the varna system, the terms "savarna" and "avarna" assumed a variety of meanings in different regions. After Indian independence, the leaders in a hurry further stamped the majority as Scheduled Tribe (ST), Scheduled Caste (SC) and Backward Caste (BC). The process of conversion for identity accelerated along with the continuing neglect of the sizable set of Indians who were stamped as Avarnas under the varna system. However, there still remains a sizable under the "Leftover." In this small island, for less than twenty years, AVP was their protector. He felt ashamed of the happenings on the mainland and tried to protect his people from the process of stamping. Only a ruler can do this. Thus, AVP could do it. The culture continues here and you can observe it."

Achachan's face glowed with extra blood. There was an unusual silence in the room. The secretary gripped the armrest of his chair. Tina and Arjun looked perplexed. The scribbling pad helped Praful and Alex to release their emotions. At the window, a small group of local people with blurred eyes waited in silence to listen to Achachan.

"Even in the recent tsunami (26 December 2004), one-third of the thuruth was submerged under water. The people here faced it boldly. As usual, government aid reached after a couple of months, when life here became normal. The island dwellers have their own methods to face natural calamity. It is our inherited skills that helped us face the natural calamity. We have a gene of self-defense. This is an example of the mighty culture. We are proud of our culture in the thuruth. We also admire people such as AVP, who could periodically add strength to such qualities. We should revive such spirit throughout the subcontinent. It is essential for the current rebuilding processes."

Achachan tried to stand up and added,

"Through this study, if we can stimulate the thinking process on the subject at different spots, like fireworks the whole subcontinent will regain its lost strength, which was unfortunately suppressed for centuries. Your studies should awaken people. If a vagabond youth is rightly led, he may do wonders. A right kind of nurturing is the need of the time to stimulate the majority stamped as Avarnas, the Leftover."

"I'll retire, as it's time for me to rest. You continue your discussions and our *vakil* will also join us."

Achachan was helped by the secretary and Ajith, who took him to Mangalam house. It was 12:40 in the afternoon, and we focused on the files kept on the table.

Praful wanted to have more time with the secretary. He said,

"Sir, we have brought lunch packets. You too should join us."

The secretary looked at his watch and said,

"My house is just nearby. And I prefer to have lunch at home at around two o' clock."

He paused and said,

"We have a canteen here. I already informed them that you will have your lunch in the canteen, and they will also supplement some items that they prepare for their usual lunch."

We had our lunch at the canteen adjoining the office. Based on our requirement, they supplemented items from their usual lunch.

When we reached the office, *vakil*, the president of the temple, was waiting for us. After the initial introductions, Praful asked him,

"Sir, based on your perception, how was the social life of the people in the thuruth and its neighborhood during the time of AVP?"

"The thuruth was like a joint family right from the time of AVP's great-grandfather." He paused, looked at the secretary and added,

"I have shared this view with many of the temple visitors. In the past, people focused more on cultivation, fishing, marketing those items, value addition and so forth. All the families participated. There was a group of thinking people, and their actions were more focused on the economic activities leading to collective welfare. However, in the neighborhood, the *Naduvazhikal* spent their time more on making laws, imposing them for looting their subjects and punishing their subjects. The process marginalized the people, and many hesitated to participate in the production process. They were isolated and they became idle. The situation created scarcity. The ignorant who wielded power further tightened the system with the introduction of more laws and taxes. Slowly, they were reduced to law-making and law-imposing groups. They lost their thinking faculty on socioeconomic development and the need for empowerment of their subjects. Exploitation was slowly inbuilt in the genes. Babies were born with added skills for exploitation. Their teachers also taught them about violence, arson and deprivation. Gods were carefully added to institutionalize the process. Fear was created among the majority and genetically imbibed, especially through women. They were kept in darkness and were never allowed empowerment. The new teachers taught and injected venomous ideas such as *Sapam* (curse), *Papam* (bad deeds), *Karma* (duties) and *Punarjanmam* (rebirth). Quality upgradation in birth was offered to institutionalize slavery. Horrifying gods, killings in temples and other vulgarities created fear psyhcosis among the people. The temple *poojaries* (priest) and *Velichappad* imposed untouchability and kept away the large majority from the wealth-generating resources such as land, labor, capital and management. Places for empowerment were converted into temples with new idols of gods and goddesses designed to quench the mythical aspirations of the people. The process weakened the majority and in the long run, their survival was like that of worms in a gutter."

Praful intervened,

"Even today, our governments are focused more on law-making. Our parliament, legislative assemblies and even local self-governments spend more time on law-making and either less time or no time on affairs related to socioeconomic development and welfare. Perhaps both the public and their elected representatives still keep the umbilical cord with the early *Naduvazhikal.* The recent atrocities and corruption of the elected representatives are clear examples of our inherited culture and the forgetting of our great past, the culture taught by our own great teachers such as Lord Buddha."

Alex raised his hand and tried to get *vakil*'s attention.

"Indians talk about a two-digit economic growth. But most of us still remain poor and dejected. We, as a research team, frequently travel to villages in different states. The majority of the villagers are observed to be under poverty level. Why does this continue even after sixty-eight years of independence and elected government? How was it possible for a person such as AVP and his predecessors to achieve the empowerment process on this small piece of land?" Why can't we replicate such success stories?' Alex queried.

Vakil's face brightened with a broad smile. He looked at Alex affectionately and said,

"We have to study this phenomenon. Researchers like you can help the public in tracing out the missing links. After independence, Indians are getting better educated but unfortunately, the educated youth are forced to migrate from their villages. They go to urban areas, and the majority gets stuck in urban slums. As a result, our local areas are not getting empowered. Our consumption increases with the new money order economy. The collective efficiency in a local area in production, value addition, trade, arts, sports, literature and even spiritual achievements either remains stagnant or gets dried up. In AVP's time, the culture in this thuruth was of a surplus economy with upgraded skills, access to new technology, trade and commerce."

"You mean, the empowerment process in the *thuruth* could continue and match with the time, whereas in many other Indian villages it was missed out on because of the long misrule? Slavery made the majority of the people unambitious and docile. They were not allowed to think and contribute in their local area. Therefore, they lagged behind in terms of overall progress. The better use of the local resources, upgrading of local skills, adoption of new technology and creation of surplus remained stagnant over centuries."

Alex looked at vakil, expecting a further explanation.

"Let us peruse what happened in the recent past in many of the rural houses in Kerala. When they were in need of money, instead of making use of the locally available rich resources, they sent their relatively smarter sons in search of jobs to Gulf countries. Their remittances, after clearing their liabilities, were invested in lands, buildings and ornaments. They were seldom invested in income-generating activities. As a result, the local resources remain idle. The smarter youth were out, and the leftover often lacked the aptitude and skills required for income generation. They became dependent, and their faculties were developed mostly to enjoy the remittances. Advantages of the development process addressed by the nation after independence were missed in the vast majority of the local areas due to the long-driven slavery-like conditions and the resultant incapability at personal and village levels." He paused and added,

'The smartest from the villages are out and they contribute outside the village, obviously being paid much better than their wage earnings. Therefore, progress takes place somewhere else. The money that reaches the villages is spent more on consumer goods, resulting in a new variety of market-led supply chains. Competition in consumerism dominates our neighborhood. In most of such households, the ones who toil outside are exploited. This is the lesson we have learned from our recent Kerala Model development. Even our *grama panchayat* fails to develop a faculty to deploy its own development funds. Large-level value degradation happened to our people due to the earlier slavery and the new emerging system. Unfortunately, the mindset still remains."

He paused and looked at Alex, who appeared as though he wanted to share something. Alex gestured vakil to continue.

"In Kerala, we see a disciplined crowd only in front of religious places and wine shops of Beverage Corporation. Correlation, if any, is a subject worth probing for you, researchers."

Alex was getting nearer to his favorite subject. The bad effects of the long misrule made the majority of the people in India inferior. The feeble threads that Alex could pick up from the *thuruth* made him realize the advantages of a less disturbed people in the island where AVP lived.

"Sir, do you mean that AVP had an advantage of inheriting a better local area and a set of less disturbed people in the island and that made him better empowered to take care of his people and to raise his voice against the misrule?" Alex asked.

Praful intervened,

"From the available history of Kerala, it is reflected that the atrocities committed by the local rajas in Travancore against the *Avarnas* were unparalleled.

Do you mean to say that such incidents did not occur in Arattupuzha, and especially in Mangalam village?"

Vakil's eyes sparkled.

"That is what surprises us! In fact, AVP was active in Mangalam for around twenty years only. Before him, the local chiefs also performed their duties. No one ever dared misrule, and no bad practices happened here. This was not accidental. Even today, the people in this *thuruth* appear to be fearless. They mix with their neighbors, and there is collective dependence. No religion-based conversion took place here. We have a church without any Christian in the *thuruth*. Like the Shiva Temple, the church is collectively maintained by us. In our day-to-day lives, people from different faiths mix with us and earn their livelihood."

Alex was in a hurry and he asked,

"Do all the people in the *thuruth* belong to the Hindu faith?"

Vakil felt comfortable answering that question. He might have often heard similar questions. He smiled and said,

"That is what you have to find out. We have a temple and a church here."

He paused and expressed his own long-felt doubt.

"Whether AVP was a believer of Hindu faith? Many people pose this question to me. I encourage them to find out the truth for themselves. When the neighboring culture suppressed the majority under the banner of Brahmanical Hinduism, why was AVP different? He could have also followed the local practices or kept silent or enjoyed the fun. But he reacted and even used physical forces to stop the atrocities. It is a long-persisting subject for all of us."

Alex wanted to share something lighter and he looked at me. I gave a go-ahead sign and he said,

"If I were AVP 150 years ago with a stunning physique, fabulous wealth, infrastructure and local support, I would have jolly well joined the *Kutty* (young) Raja's club. It gives us an opportunity for a wildlife experience at the cost of the oppressed."

"Yes, almost everyone will use power for personal gain and enjoyment. Our Indian rajas were notorious for doing the same. In such a context, a different kind of behavior is strange. Perhaps, our collective efforts will throw some light on the subject—Why AVP was different?"

Praful tried to come out of the subject.

"Maybe in each one of us there is a value-based hidden culture; a culture taught by Puthanachan, Lord Buddha. In the genes of AVP and his clan, the opportunity to dilute them was perhaps less and therefore, they behaved like Buddhists, the enlightened," he added and looked at vakil, who was looking at his watch.

❋❋❋

Praful looked at his watch again and said,

"We can have another fifteen minutes and we may discuss specific points."

Alex took the opportunity, looked at the president and the secretary and said,

"We have heard about AVP's role in promoting various arts, especially Kathakali. Will you be able to brief us on what AVP did for promoting arts and culture in Arattupuzha?"

The secretary prompted the president and he said,

"You may be well aware of the origin of Kathakali. Its different forms exist in most of the countries where Buddhism flourishes. In neighboring Sri Lanka, it is popular under its local name, perhaps *Ves*. In Kerala, it was known as *Attam* and it was a silent dance drama using well-codified footwork, finger poses, eye and facial muscle movements; it involved the use of a sign language to spread the teachings of the great masters to the common flock in and around the Viharas and the Pallies during the earlier period. Later, as an entertainment, it was played in temples during night hours in front of a large oil-lit lamp that was popularly known as *Attavilakku* in Kerala. The locally available drums were used for creating a festive mood, and skillful artists performed Attom before a selected audience in newly developed religious seats and residences of the powerful. Earlier, as the dialects varied from place to place, the sign language and the local instruments were used for announcement and for communicating vital information among the Patikramas and local habitats. The art form got rooted in Kerala due to the long-term influence of Buddhist culture, friendly climate, rich agriculture, large leisure time and, subsequently, through the patronage of the newly emerging local chiefs. Hundreds of *Attam* clubs flourished in Kerala during that time along with the local *Kalari* and *Asan* schools. The large concept of Gurukulam got established in local areas with the help of sign language; communication of local knowledge and the the common man was benifitted through this form of entertainment, and this system slowly got institutionalized. This further strengthened the spread of Viharas, Chaithyas, Gurukulams, later *Kalaris* and *Asan* schools. It appears as a large institutional change program through time and is based on sociopolitical changes. A shift from the knowledge-based institutions to establishments based on muscle power and spreading of mythology can be further observed. These subjects are worthy for further research. The process of change also happened in the *thuruth*. But the ardent nature of the local people to cling to their earlier values can be still observed. People like AVPs, I think, had a larger role throughout the subcontinent in preserving and protecting the mighty culture, a culture addressing empowerment of the common man based on science, technology and skill formation."

"Why did AVP have to reintroduce the same in his island?" Alex, as usual, raised a doubt.

"Perhaps the restrictions imposed by Savarnas on the large majority might have made the art form a privileged one for them and for a short period, they could deny its access to the public, just like the restrictions they had imposed on learning, mobility, access to temples and streets, wearing clothes and ornaments. The island too might have faced its own isolation due to the restriction on mobility of the artists from the mainland. And when AVP got the opportunity under the fast-changing scenario of colonial rule, he took advantage of it and reintroduced the missing links. The establishment of the Shiva Temple also might have served as a platform for the rebuilding process. This is one of the reasons for us to protect the local people and to showcase their culture to the world as a specimen of our rich past. We had discussed this point with Prof Bala many times, and your Achachan has perhaps lived up to this time to witness the youth taking over this subject for in-depth studies. We feel that we could live up to our expectations and the future is safe in the hands of the upcoming generation. The realization of our limitations and the internalization of corrective measures are symptoms of the survival of our better gene. It is time to realize and internalize the process of change. The changes will lead us to experience the feeling of enlightenment, as physically felt on a Deewali day," vakil said.

Praful probed further,

"Sir, we are curious to know more about the role played by AVP in empowering the local people with an infrastructure such as the Siva Temple, *Attam* Club, *Kalari* and *Asan* schools, but which have faded out due to the misrule."

Vakil took time to reply. He smiled at Praful and said,

"Like you people, AVP was a brilliant social scientist. He carefully studied the timely needs of the people and reintroduced them one by one to meet local requirements. He remained a student throughout his life. When the people in the *thuruth* felt the need for a temple, he neither consulted any one nor sought permission. He went to Pazhani, the famous Murugan Temple, Gokarnam, Kanyakumari and Vaikom; stayed in those famous temples as a devotee and learned the systems related to temple construction and the daily rituals. His six-feet-plus Homeric figure enabled him to get into those temples, stay there and study them like a sociologist who was involved in participant observations. He was very shrewd in reading the mind of temple authorities and spent money lavishly to gain their support. It is said that two of his escorts who waited outside such temples were often shocked to see AVP return from the temple with a few temple men respectfully escorting him and inviting him for another visit with their family members. It is said that he had an athletic body and an extraordinary pleasing face with radiant eyes. His movement and gestures were the most rhythmic, and his voice was masculine. He always wore fine mal-mal dhothies with thin golden borders and covered his body with another finely woven *narieth* (upper garment) through which his golden chain with pearls and a diamond pendant were visible. He always wore brown leather shoes with two-inch heels, and these produced an unusual soft sound when he walked. It is said that horse grains were carefully stuffed by the shoemaker into the shoes to ensure the fabulous sound. He was very particular about this way of dressing. He also insisted on his escort wearing clothes that matched his own. He marched elegantly along with his escorts. He loved the display and used it as a social tool to ensure social justice."

"Then what happened? Did anyone catch him?" Alex was curious.

"This went on until one day at the Vaikom Temple when a few priests politely enquired about his caste. He pleasantly told them in their own privately used internal dialect that they may carry out the purification, and he gave them the normal charges for purification along with double the amount as tips. The clergymen waved goodbye and requested him to visit the temple frequently so that this disciple of the Lord could bring fortune to them as well."

He paused and said,

"As per our temple records, he befriended a practitioner called Viswanathan Gurukkal hailing from Kandiyoor Madam at Mavelikkara. With his active association, AVP established the Shiva Temple at Mangalam on 6 Medam 1029 Malayalam Calendar (1854 AD). The daily *poojas* were carried out in the temple by the willing priestly class during the initial stages. Yearly celebrations were also organized as per the desires of the people. It is currently known as *Mangalam Idakkad Janeswara Keshetram*." He paused.

"Did AVP face any difficulties in the establishment of the temple?" Praful asked.

"No, there was no confrontation with anybody in the *thuruth* for establishing the temple. Perhaps, the location of the *thuruth* and the interest of the local people enabled AVP to succeed in such a venture. It is said that a few Savarnars complained to the local ruler Chempakasery, and AVP gave a befitting reply that he had established the temple for the local people, known as *Ezhavas*, based on their need to worship their Puthanachan, currently in vogue as Shivan, and not Savarna's Shivan! Therefore, they had no need to worry about their gods, who were safe in their own respective temples."

Praful intervened,

"Why did AVP go in for a temple rather than a Chaithya, an empowerment center related to the larger culture of the Leftover in India?"

Vakil was again lost in his thoughts. Looking at Praful, he said,

"I'm unable to answer this question. Perhaps, now we can talk on reviving the lost culture. Maybe leaders like Ms Mayavathi, former Chief Minister of Uttar Pradesh, has shown the guts to speak openly on the need for the revival process and initiated the empowerment of the 'Leftover' in her state. Perhaps AVP had satisfied the wishes of his loving people by constructing a temple. Or he himself might have been a worshipper of Lord Shiva, on whom the virtues of Lord Buddha were superimposed under the Brahmanical reengineering processes."

He paused, looked at all of us and continued,

"The choice of Lord Shiva appears to me the best alternate to Lord Buddha, their loving Puthanachan of Odanadu. This sort of a preference is also shown by Jagath Guru Sree Narayana in the famous installation of the Shiva Temple at Aruvipuram after a lag of fifty-seven years. During his educational days, Jagath Guru was at Onattukara and was attached to the traditional school at Varanappally. Jagath Guru might have visited Mangalam Temple a few times during his higher-level education and might have drawn from the basic needs for the institutionalization process of the less privileged. The Leftover and the temple might have been used as instruments to organize the people and to readress their issues on a collective and common platform."

Alex intervened,

"There appears to be a long delay in the revival process. Will you please explain the cause of delay in your area, especially after AVP's initiation?"

"Perhaps, the fear psychosis prevailing didn't permit them; or, whether it was due to some other hidden factors, only time will tell. Researchers will have a larger role to play in tracing out the facts. Even the converts who got themselves relatively better empowered also kept aloof from the Leftover. As a result, both Brahmanism and Buddhism were weekend. Even the converts and their leaders failed to address the collective common welfare of the larger public. Like the current market competition, the sellers pushed their own products in the market. In the process, we forget to address the much-needed welfare of humanity," vakil explained.

Alex appeared still confused. He was unknowingly on his feet, perhaps, with the probing mind of a researcher. He was a brilliant student from Sri Lanka, and he had successfully completed his M Phil and PhD at Delhi University before attaining twenty-six years of age. When he was confused, he preferred to stand. Praful, who was familiar with his habits, neglected his posture. Others were enjoying the scene. He stood there in front of us, biting his pen, often scribbling and reflecting a face that was often totally lost and regained.

❀❀❀

"Sir, we have a plan to walk around the island and see for ourselves the place, its settings, the habitat and the life. It is now 3:30 in the afternoon. We would love to be on the island till the sun sets and then return to Mangalam house. We would certainly like both of you to spend some time with us at Manglam house after eight o' clock." Praful looked at both the president and the secretary of the temple.

The car was around. We could hear Ajith Chettan, and he came in.

"Both of us will meet you before your return to Delhi. Bala will reach on Friday; during the evening hours of that day, all of us would come to Mangalam house to meet our childhood friend."

The president smiled at us and looked at Ajith, who was passing signals to Praful regarding the usual evening party. Seeing the gestures, we all laughed and those who stood at the window joined us. Alex got distracted and he struggled to make out the reasons for our snigger.

"Now, it is more than thirty years that Bala is in Delhi. Before his marriage, such vacations were really adventurous for us. We used to spend most of the time in the *thuruth,* fishing, playing, swimming and rowing. When hungry, we got into one of the nearby houses and ate. There was no formality, and we had no shyness. When I joined defense service, our vacations were planned, and bottles from the defense canteen adored the earlier toddy-cum-tapioca-cum-fish delicacies. When Bala started travelling abroad, duty-free bottles also joined us along with Bala's favorite duck fry. Ajith is an expert in making duck fry. You people should make use of his talent before leaving this place."

The president gave us tips and added,

"Let me see whether our canteen is ready for the tea."

*Vakil* looked at his watch and slowly walked towards the canteen.

Ajith was already with his support services as usual and shouted from the window,

"Tea-coffee and *parippuvada* (oil-fried Kerala delicacy prepared with pulses, spring onion, red chillies and spices) is ready. Please come to the canteen. They are waiting for us."

I got out of the room and walked through the temple compound. Tina followed. The white sand still had evidence of the day's heat. A few girls were seen collecting the fallen flowers from *Ezhachempakam* (Ipomoea) next to the ladies wash at the northern corner. We refreshed ourselves, joined the small group of girls and ladies and exchanged pleasantries. An elderly lady scolded me for keeping my hair open in the temple compound. She came near me and without my consent plaited my hair. The girls around giggled.

We looked at the Ezhachempakam. It was full of buds waiting to bloom during the night. Those flowers had ivory white petals that were tinged with golden yellow. Their slight fragrance filled the evening air. We collected a few flowers from the girls and walked towards the canteen.

The canteen smelled of hot *parippuvada*. I kept the flowers on the table, and we took our share of v*ada* and coffee.

"Chippy, do you know the importance of this flower?" the secretary asked.

I looked at Praful and then at Alex.

"Yes, it was brought by us; the Sri Lankans who came to India and the Buddhist monks planted them in their Viharas and Chaithyas."

Alex looked at the secretary, who was in appreciation of Alex and said,

"Yes, Alex is right. You can see the plant in a few Kerala temples and houses in Onattukara. Unfortunately, it was chopped off by vested interests and the people were even scared by the spreading of stories that such plants are the abode of devils, demons and *gandharvans*."

"But in this *thuruth*, I have seen this tree in a few houses," Alex said.

"Yes, in the *thuruth*, it is still there. But in the neighborhood, on the mainland, it is rarely seen." Looking at vakil, the secretary added,

"When Bala comes, we all love to sit beneath the tree, especially during moonlit nights, and talk. Its fragrance at night is beyond words. It has to be felt."

I enjoyed the *chukku* (dry ginger) coffee and *parippuvada*. It was crisp and yummy. Ajith Chettan sometimes brings foodstuff that emits a pungent smell and contains prawns inside, especially for their get-together parties. Perhaps he will bring it next Friday for Bala uncle and his company.

Ajith Chettan started the car and waited for us. Praful was still talking with the temple people. I approached them and listened.

"Sir, we have only three days left to complete our work. Achachan gives us company only upto the lunch hours. Will you join us during our visits to the nearby areas?"

The president looked at the secretary and said,

"It is summer holidays for the court. But I have to attend to my office work because of certain earlier appointments. Therefore, I can be with you only after 2:00 in the afternoon."

Praful looked at the secretary and he readily agreed to be with the team till the lunch hours. It was a relief to Praful and could be read from his face.

"We love to see the places related to Buddhism, such as Ambalappuzha, Harippad, Mannarasala and Ochira, if possible, by tomorrow," Praful said.

Walking nearer to the car, Praful and Alex thanked them. We got into the car. I felt deeply indebted to the secretary and the president. Sitting in the front seat, I folded my hands as a mark of respect to them. The secretary came nearer to me and whispered,

"Let Bala come along with those Delhi *bhaiyas*. It is time for us to pull your ears."

Both of them laughed. I smiled and waved at them.

# 4

## *Arattupuzha and AVP*

The car took a left turn from the main road. The evening sun was stronger and it made the air more humid. We all longed for a fast drive to welcome the sea breeze.

Ajith Chettan commented,

"It might rain at night. Look at those clouds! It will be the first shower of this monsoon."

Suddenly, I felt the absence of Tina and Arjun in the car. I said,

"Let us move to the bridge first. Tina and Arjun will be waiting for us."

I didn't like Tina getting drenched at Mangalam in the company of Arjun. The car picked up speed. I missed Neeraj. It was going to be the first shower of the incoming monsoon.

Why did our secretary want to pull my ears? These elders can even smell the rats hiding in Delhi. No, there is no chance to know about Neeraj, I tried to defend myself, made up a smile and looked for Tina and Arjun.

"We can see only the sea. Where is the river?" Alex said, breaking the silence.

"Shall I take you to the river side?" Ajith asked. He could follow both English and Hindi.

"Yes, we would like to see two or three places at each side. It is better that we drive up to the bridge, collect our friends and while returning we shall stop at a few places. Both Chippy and Ajith can choose the places," Praful said.

The Innova car and Ajith Chettan were familiar in the *thuruth*. On the way, people waved at Ajith Chettan and he reciprocated and exchanged pleasantries. The assembly elections were just held and people were waiting for the results and perhaps there was an added silence on the street. The sea took full advantage of the same.

We could spot Tina and Arjun a few meters ahead of us. I asked Ajith Chettan to quietly follow them. Both Praful and Alex understood the whispers in Malayalam and I could make them chase the victim like James Bond 007 on a secret mission. They were walking slowly and occasionally their hands were tempting to touch each other. There was no threat of monsoon rains over their heads. Their only wish appeared to be a never-ending road to the bridge.

Alex whispered something to Ajith; he drove the car silently, reached behind Tina and Arjun and blew the horn. To our surprise, Arjun held Tina's wrist tightly and both of them turned towards to face us. It was a show to the passersby, and they chuckled heartily.

"Arjun knows her thoroughly and he will never leave her. His reaction was spontaneous," Praful said.

I felt the same. Tina has made the right choice. What about me? That fellow's mind, I could never read. There can be a murder if he fails to ring me today, I thought.

Tina and Arjun got in and the car gained speed, reaching the new bridge connecting Mangalam to the main road.

We got down from the car at a unique spot. Nature has its own fencing arrangement to protect the tiny *thuruth*. The thick vegetative cover near us showcased nature's skill and her fabulous design. The man-made bridge at the corner appeared like a band-aid on a broken limb.

It was 5:00 in the evening, and the sun was still aggressive. Praful filled his writing pad, and Alex took snaps. Praful called us to listen to him.

"We all will move to the river side. Each one will note down their own observation without any discussion. If we can cover two or three pockets from each side, the river and the sea side, we may be able to draw basic information that is required for preparing the project proposal. Before sunset, we can wind up."

We took our scribbling pads along and followed Praful and Ajith Chettan.

First, we approached a fishermen hamlet near the seashore. A good number of traditional canoes, a few fiber glass canoes, fishing nets and fish trays were on the shore. At a distance, a few fishermen and their family members were picking up sardines from their fishing nets. Silver-colored sardines are called *Mathy* in Malayalam. Blue plastic trays were used to store the fish. The group had two full trays of fish, and the third one was being filled. Our team members talked to a few fishermen.

The fishermen's houses were *pacca*. Most of them had concrete roofs, two to three rooms with a separate kitchen and a toilet. Modern gadgets such as freezer, television, mixer, two-wheeler and so on were common in the houses visited. The family members appeared healthy and happy. The children attended the local school. Fish processing, which was reported to be popular earlier, was not observed. The fishermen spend on an average three to four hours for fishing using their traditional canoes. Mechanised fishing vessels and canoes using Out Board Motors were not found.

Fishermen carrying out fishing operations in the river operated mostly during night hours to catch *karimeen* (Pearlspot), a favored fish variety in Kerala with high market demand. They used small traditional canoes, and the crew constituted only two or three fishermen. They returned to the fish-landing docks early in the morning and immediately sold those freshwater fish in an auction. Hoteliers and market operators purchased them and therefore, they were not available in the local markets for the common buyer. The cell phones enabled the fishermen to share information on their fish catch, and bulk buyers bought them in the auction. The system functioned smoothly.

The scribbling exercise and the visits continued till the sunset. We covered eight fishermen, three farmers and two petty traders. We reached Mangalam house at 7:20 in the night, completely tired. Praful is a known taskmaster, and the day's last leg reflected his professional seriousness. He collected the notes with our initials on them, and we retired to our rooms.

I went to the kitchen with Tina. The smell of *unniappam* (a Kerala delicacy made with a fermented mix of rice powder, jaggery, plantain, cardamom and coconut bits) filled the kitchen. As usual, Achamma was in her chair, away from the gas stove.

"Both of you, first take a bath and then serve these items to all. They will be hungry. We will have dinner after 8:00 in the night."

I went and held Achamma from behind and whispered,

"That is why Achachan always calls you judge."

After grabbing a few unniappams, I ran out of the kitchen, dragging Tina. She was struggling with the unniappam already in her mouth.

Smart girl, I thought. Before I could think, she does. I've already submitted my M Phil thesis to JNU. She is yet to begin. But she moves jolly well with her fiancé in a village such as Mangalam!

After freshening up, we assembled in the drawing room. Achachan, Achamma, Unniappams and the Mangalam special black coffee were waiting for us. Black coffee made with dry ginger and pepper was a better match with unniappam. The hot coffee had the power to clear the oil in our throats.

Praful briefed Achachan on the day's program and tried to schedule tomorrow's programs. He said,

"Our return ticket is for the coming Sunday. Prof Bala and his family will reach on Friday. If we wind up our field program on Thursday, we can spend the rest of the days with Prof Bala as per his schedule."

"If it is so, why don't you call your wife and son to spend a few days with you here? They will also get an opportunity to be with us and to see the places around here. It will also be a break from Delhi's scorching sun. Since Bala is leaving Delhi by Friday morning's flight, they can also join them and Ajith will pick them up from Nedumbassery airport. As your wife is in IRS, she can arrange the return ticket by train on any convenient day."

Achachan looked at Praful.

Praful was in confusion. He tried to contact his wife over the phone.

Drawing their attention, Achachan said,

"We have a family function on Sunday morning. All of you should attend and enable to make the function a grand success. Such occasions are once in a blue moon. I am happy that the youth from different parts of India and even the neighboring Sri Lanka can participate."

Looking at Alex, Achachan reconfirmed, "Am I right Alex?"

"Yes sir," Alex answered, "I was born and brought up in Sri Lanka, at 127, Union Place, Colombo.My father is the noted gynecologist Dr Raja Rathnam. My mother is from the nearby Thiruvalla. They met at Crescent Hospital in New York and are currently practicing at Colombo. My mother, Dr Lisy, has specialized in community medicine. The war-torn economy of Sri Lanka needs their services, and both of them are currently in Jaffna. So I'm definitely a Sri Lankan, your neighbor, sir."

"Are you talking about the same Dr Raja Rathnam, the world-famous gynecologist who was honored by the British Queen with knighthood?"

"Yes sir, he is my father. My mother is one of the most active doctors in community medicine in Sri Lanka."

Achachan stood on his heels and said,

"Son, you have graced our home. It is due to the good deeds of our forefathers that we get the opportunity to serve you, the young researchers."

He extended his hands. Alex went nearer to him. Achachan lifted his face and kissed him on the forehead.

We all were on our heels. Mani Aka stood there with her kitchen tool in hand and struggled to make out what was happening.

It took time to revert to the subject. Loading the unniappam in his hand, Praful told Achachan,

"My wife and son will be here on Friday with Prof Bala and family. She will arrange the return trip by Rajadhani or Kerala Express."

Achachan smiled and said,

"It's a great opportunity to meet your wife and son. With the help of your wife, I will also get a chance to update my information on the Indian Railways."

Praful was happy. Picking up a few more unniappam, he said,

"We plan to leave tomorrow to Ambalappuzha by 8:30 in the morning. Ajith told me that while returning we can visit Mannarassala and Harippad Temple. Then, we shall visit Oachira and the temple at Thrikkunnapuzha. These places have a connection with AVP, Sreemulavasam and Buddhism and are therefore important to our larger project."

"It's OK; we shall also take a smaller car," Achachan said. Then, looking at Ajith, he added,

"You may tell Lazar to bring the Maruti from Chippy's place. While coming, he can pick up our secretary."

Turning to Praful, he said,

"Tomorrow, I will be with you till lunchtime."

"Sir, can we now discuss more on AVP's social activities?" Praful asked.

"I'm ready. What about these kids? Do they want to join us? Or move around?"

❊❊❊

Praful looked at us. Alex nodded in favor, and we all sat around Achachan. The remaining unniappams also tempted us to circle around. The antique ceiling fan with its larger dome ensured pleasant circulation of air. The *nilavilakku* (oil lamp) kept in front of Jagath Guru enabled the night to have appropriate setting for closer discussions.

"To me, the 150 years that had prevailed in Onattukara had molded AVP. Denial of personal freedom by the ignorant local chiefs, silent support to them by the Royal family of Travancore and the cunning colonial rulers made a mess of the situation. On the one side, fast-advancing technologies and application of the same and on the other side cultural lag to access them by the so-called rulers made them feel inferior. The mounting inferiority complex of the rulers might have narrowed down their thinking faculty and it resulted in continuous harassment of their own subjects through the introduction of new laws and regulations. The process alienated the majority of the people in the subcontinent and even in the tiny Onattukara from their rulers."

"Sir, you were mentioning the inferiority complex of the local rulers and the larger public. Can you please further elaborate?" Alex appealed.

"If I'm in a group and poorly dressed, don't know the etiquette of that group, am unable to speak the language that the elite speak, fail to understand the subjects they talk and my own people are their menial servants, I'll feel inferior and develop a fear psychosis. If I don't have guts, I can never kick the Johnys around. Our *naduvazhikal* (local rulers) also felt the same way. A similar complex is still experienced by many of us. If we can dress properly and effectively communicate in English, the majority of the crowd around us would develop certain complexes, even today. I think that over time this has become a hidden genetic factor among us. However, AVP was different, totally different from the local chiefs of Onattukara during his time."

"Whether it was the superiority complex of AVP that made him different?" Alex asked.

"Can we call that complex as the true culture of the local people?"

Achachan smiled at Alex and asked,

"Why do you Alex, at this young age, dissect this grand old man to know the truth?"

Again with a broad smile and sparkling eyes, Achanchan looked at Alex and said,

"The rich culture you inherited from your parents, a Buddhist father and a Christian mother and being born and brought up in one of the rich cultural seats, Colombo, will reflect a matured cultural quality. Your mother, who hails from Thiruvalla and is working in a medical profession, perhaps may have a larger cultural background inherited from Thiruvalla, where a large number of medical professionals are actively engaged in the medical profession throughout the world." Achachan again smiled at Alex and he added,

"My loving son, your curiosity itself can be genetically acquired. Pursue the same, and you will be able to connect the lost Buddhist convent at Malikappuram, near Sabarimala, with the skilled and beautiful girls of Thiruvalla who take care of the millions of suffering people throughout the world!"

Alex intervened, "Sir, is it not due to the economic reasons that they opt for medical professions?"

"No, definitely not," Achachan said. He smiled and continued,

"There are other professions through which they can make money, even at Thiruvalla. It has rich natural resources and they are capable of using these resources. A few also argue that it is the Church that supports them. It is true that the Church has a major role in their training and placement. I feel that if the Church used better organizational connectivity, it would be able to perfect the inherent qualities of the Thiruvalla girls. Otherwise, why are similar features less reflected in Christian-dominated and comparable local areas both within India and abroad?"

"Sir, it appears to be an important subject for social scientists for further research. I have heard of Thiruvalla girls' contributions in the medical field. During my college days, there was a popular joke that in the hospitals of the United States, the language commonly heard during night time was Malayalam," Praful commented.

"Even the second and third generations of these Indians have spread over to the entire world and many of them are currently specialized doctors, scientists and other professionals. These are the legacy of a larger culture inherited by us due to the collective efforts and hard work of those brilliant teachers who served us during the 1,000-year period, on which we have limited information. If we have the patience to look into these missing aspects, forgetting our menial rift, we can bring out many of our strengths," Achachan added.

Looking at us, he continued,

"All economies try to strengthen the institution-building process. But many a time, we neglect those institutions that our forefathers had developed for our collective welfare and we are on the lookout for the new and at times, the unknown. During our time, the greatest evil we face is corruption in all walks of our life. If we focus on our own past, we can sort out social instruments to address such issues. Inspite of the police, judiciary, vigilance, anticorruption bureaus, various auditing systems, self-declaration methods, oath-taking ceremonies, the Lok Pal Bill and so on, the issue still persists. It also spreads amid us, like cancer. Perhaps the earlier lessons we learned on finding eternal happiness, if reintroduced, updated and practiced in the current context, may address the issue."

"Sir, Bertrand Russel says: Man's fear is responsible for superstitions and one of the main causes for cruelty. To conquer fear is the beginning of wisdom and only the enlightened can lead us. The large-level conversion to Christianity can be one of the reasons for retaining its rich culture. The Brahmanism left in Thiruvalla and its surrounding places was based on human values; perhaps, this had happened due to the true Buddhist culture of the local area. The absence of a similar culture in other comparable Brahmanical pockets in Kerala and elsewhere in India will perhaps support Achachan's views. Anyway, by careful studies of the people's habits, practices and culture prevailing during our own time, we can arrive at valid conclusions," Praful said.

"During the long forty years of my service in the Indian Railways, I had the opportunity to work in different places in southern states. Among the Malayalees who had settled outside Kerala, the people of Thiruvalla dominate in organizing Malayalee forums and cultural festivities, especially during Onam, Christmas and the New Year. Perhaps, a relatively better and imbibed cultural trait can be the reason for their initiatives."

Achachan shared his experience as a retired general manager of the mighty Indian Railway.

Standing behind Achachan, his wife murmured. Perhaps, she was intolerant of the long time that the research team was availing of her husband. It was only after forty years of long waiting that she could get him out from the Indian Railway.

Mani Akka kept a plastic chair for Achamma just behind her husband. It was an indication that the dinner was ready. Achamma would have her usual shower and would soon join the group.

Mani Akka also made herself comfortable nearer to me. Achachan loves their presence and will never miss an opportunity to involve them in such discussions. Achachan looked back at the empty chair and continued,

"During the time of AVP also, land-based economic activities predominated. Only a few were engaged in trade and commerce. Value addition by grading, sorting, packing and marketing was less developed during those times. Agro-processing was rarely practiced. Fish drying and milk processing for *ghee* (clarified butter) were familiarized but others like textiles, color dyeing, salt making etc. were not familiar in Onattukara. land was abducted by the savarna and was classified under *pandaramvaka, sripandaramvaka, kandukrishi, sreepadam* lands and so forth. The laws on the ownership of land were shaped by the Savarnas and were implemented through the local chiefs and the people who were stamped as sudhras, their supporters. There was no judicial system in Travancore. Only in 1861, the British civil and criminal procedure codes were introduced and, subsequently, the first Jail at Quilon (Kollam) was established.

The *Naduvazhikal* confirmed the punishments based on the local *maryada* or customs. The Savarnas promoted a system that all the lands belonged to God and that they were the entrusted custodians of God himself. Seizing the land from the local farmers became a regular practice of the savarna with the help of their so-called army consisting of the newly raised sudhras. At one point, AVP developed a self-defensive method to check the intrusion of this culture in his *thuruth*. He was even ready to use physical power to check the spreading of the malicious practices. A school of thought emerged under his leadership to resist such intrusion.' Achachan paused and looked at Praful. Before he could react, Alex had drawn his attention. He said,

"Sir, it is heard that AVP's interference had created a wave in Onattukara to check the Savarnas from looting the matured crops."

Achachan smiled and said,

"Like the earlier folklore and the present media, you too want sensational stories!"

He looked at Praful and Arjun. Tina was almost lying on the carpet, cuddling with a round pillow. It is likely that before dinner itself she will fall asleep, I guessed.

Achachan continued,

"In those days, under nonregistered land, *porampoke*, *tharisu* and land under reserved forests dominated. There was a place called Maha Devi Kadu near our *thuruth*, on the western side of Karthikapally taluk. The local people cultivated a variety of crops in their land for the longest time. Under the changed land tenure system, one imported savarna family, a *Potty* was transplanted to the village and they made a royal or divine claim of the entire land. The poor farmers were unable to digest the emerging system. The henchmen of the *Potty's* family moved to the field and collected the best crops based on their requirements using *Potty's name*. One farmer called Kesavan took a few fellow farmers and placed the issue before AVP. He studied the severity of the subject and then posted half a dozen men to guard the field. When the Potty's henchmen reached, they were caught and their hands and legs were tied; they were wrapped in their own *dhothies* and virtually kept for public display on the specially erected frame near a vegetable garden, where mature snake gourds were hanging in plenty. The scene, it is said, created such humor in the village that a few complained of upturned tummies due to unchecked guffaw. The Potty, who came to witness the scene, ran for his life. He didn't like to be hanging amid the snake gourds. People nicknamed farmer Kesavan as Kesavan Potty. The real Potty silently agreed to the existing system much before the elected Communist Government in Kerala enacted its Land Reform Act in favor of the tillers. It is said that the real *Potty* had subsequently became a gentleman Potty and maintained friendly relations with AVP and his neighboring farmers. The *Potty* might have subsequently enjoyed the humor created by AVP."

Tina stood up, lifted her round pillow, hung it like a snakegourd and shouted,

"Can we imagine our loving *Potty* in such a position?" All giggled and Achachan continued,

"The time was conducive for stealing and looting by using the self-drawn privileges. One Patchu Menon at Mambuzhakara in Kuttanad, which is half an hour drive from our *thuruth*, developed an unusual fancy in forcefully taking away better-yielding and newly calved cows from the poor people. He took a high-yielding cow and its calf from his own *Vaidya*, the medical practitioner. The *Vaidya* was a scholarly person and he kept silent even after a week. When AVP came to know about the incident, he reached the place in his *theethuppi* (canoe speeding like fire) with his commandos and loaded the cow and calf into the canoe. It is said that AVP whispered something into the ears of Menon and his fellowmen burst into laughter. When AVP was about to step into his canoe, Menon's daughter handed over a loving lamb to AVP and requested him to accept it as a compensation for the crime that her father had committed. Kissing her forehead, AVP asked the commandos to hand it over to *Vaidya* as a token of love from Menon's daughter. It is said that the girl clung on to AVP's hand like his own daughter would."

Alex was impatient again and he asked,

"Achachan, what was the murmur that made Menon's fellowmen to laugh at such a tense situation?"

Achachan laughed, pushed his wife who was sitting near him and said,

"You are a *badmash* (mischievous). Can't you ask such a thing privately?" Achachan chuckled.

"Okay, it was guessed by the commandos that AVP reminded Menon of the presence of the strong bulls at Oachira that can make even Menon pregnant if he again develops such a desire for others' newly calved cows."

He added, "It was also heard that the people in that locality boycotted Menon and his daughter had to persuade AVP to restart their services. In fact, AVP had no personal enemity and he was only against the system that advocated malpractices."

Praful drew Achachan's attention and said,

"Sir, I read that AVP was punished for breaking laws. Can you please elaborate that incident?"

"During his time, there was a custom that when a Savarna moves through the main street, his or her group will shout 'ohy…ohy.' The sound warns the approach of a Savarna and the Avarna should move away by maintaining the stipulated distance. Or else, they will be beaten and punished. The system was practiced by certain *Naduvazhies,* who were mostly ignorant. In the *Thuruth*, however, 'ohy…ohy' was never heard. Once AVP and his group were moving on a public street from Thrikkunnapuzha to Pulikeezhu. From the opposite side, the son of Edapally Raja was coming with his group. Seeing AVP and his group, they shouted 'ohy…ohy.' AVP and group shouted back, making a frightening noise. Both parties met face to face and that resulted in pushing and pulling. Before the champions of martial arts, the poor prince and his group had to eat the mud of the paddy field. The incident infuriated Edapally Raja. He filed a suit before the Court of Travancore, and AVP and his group members were punished with one-year imprisonment. But the incident opened the eyes of the then privileged and they totally stopped 'ohy…ohy' in Onattukara. When AVP and his group were released from the jail, the people in Onattukara mimicked 'ohy…ohy,' and it was celebrated by the young and the old. A large number of Savarnas also joined the public meetings to ridicule the wrongdoing. The sound vibrations in the meeting subdued 'ohy…ohy' forever in Onattukara. Only mischievous children running through the paddy field in Onattukara mimicked 'ohy…ohy' thereafter."

Achachan smiled and added,

"To all of you, it may look quite unbelievable. Today, things have changed. 'We need men who can dream of things that were never there,' John F. Kennedy, the late President of the United States used to insist. Perhaps, in this *thuruth*, we were lucky to get the leadership of a legendary figure such as AVP. He might not have received any support from the then prevailing social system. Then, who had inspired him? In Indian history, only Lord Buddha empowered the public through trained teachers and further institutionalized the process. Can we say that the AVP's gene might have inherited such traits from the larger culture that we lost?"

Achamma gestured to her husband that it was time for dinner. Mani Akka, who was sitting behind me, had already withdrawn to the kitchen.

"All of you may assemble at the dining table and we can have further discussions there."

It was Achamma's verdict. That is why she was called "judge" by Achachan and secretly by others. This judge is ruling Mangalam house for the past sixty-eight years, I thought and smiled.

We met at the dining table. North Indian dishes dominated. Achachan had his usual *podiyari kanji* (broken rice gruel) and green gram. Both husband and wife are well tuned to such a menu as per my memory. Often, we children were also given these two items and Bala uncle and my brother used to protest by threatening to go on a temporary hunger strike. Achamma had the skill of handling them with egg fries, which were specially made with two eggs of the locally available ducks.

Tina was the first one to register her appreciation of Mani Akka's skill to make excellent *chapathy* (rolled bread), *daal* (mashed pulse curry) and *bhindi* fry (fried ladies' fingers). Tasting them, she said,

"Each item tasted like its authentic form. We should abduct her to JNU, as a faculty under our faculty improvement program."

"She had been to Delhi twice and Kochamma too had taught her a few Punjabi and Gujarati dishes. She can prepare baigan–ka–bhartha (Punjabi dish) and undhio (Gujarati dish) excellently. When Bala uncle and his family are here, you can really enjoy her culinary skills," I added.

Mani Akka moved around with her sensor and software for translation. Its fun when she narrates such episodes to her husband, first in broken English and then their translation in Malayalam. Ajith Chettan would listen to the whole story like a priest patiently listening to a new *kumbasaram* (confession).

As usual, Achamma, Ajith Chettan and Mani Akka also joined the dinner table. After the second service, they usually join with the guest. Achachan is very particular about Ajith Chettan and Mani Akka's joining the family members for dinner. When there is no guest, Achachan will insist on them joining during the first service itself. Mani Akka keeps herself always in a presentable form to join the different groups.

After a break of half an hour, we reassembled in the drawing room as directed by Praful. We had a quick review of the day's work and planned to leave for Ambalappuzha by 8:30 in the morning.

# 5

## Sreemoolavasam

### The Submerged Buddhist Seat of Learning & Empowerment

The traffic on NH47 was slowly picking up. The drive to Ambalappuzha Sreekrishna Swami Temple usually takes less than an hour from Mangalam. The morning breeze was refreshing. Activities on the sides of the road and the visibility of the sea at certain points from the road kept us united with mother earth. Her mischievous children were yet to spoil her long, outstretched beach. Both wind and waves kept it clean.

We reached in front of the temple at around 9:15 in the morning.

Achachan, the secretary, and Ajith Chettan went to the beautiful *melkettu* (balcony) near the temple pond. Facing us, Achachan said,

"We will wait here. You go around the temple compound and also have the *darshan*. We will talk about the temple and its surrounding places after your *dharshan*. Take one of the local guides' help, or even Chippy can guide you. There are a few books about the temple. It will be helpful for probing your favorite subject, the Leftover." He smiled and went inside the *melkettu*, the viewer's place. It was a massive structure facing the large temple pond. The smooth flow of the wind from the pond extended a warm welcome to visitors.

Tina and Arjun were already on the move. We three followed them. The temple compound was large, silent and serene. In its *pattambalam* (prayer hall), a few visitors were found relaxing. Tina and Arjun talked to an elderly couple in English.

"Let us find out a bookseller. Perhaps Chippy will be able to choose a couple of books that are useful to us." Praful led us to the *pattambalam*. Alex, with his broken Malayalam, approached an elderly person with a shoulder bag who took out half a dozen books from his bag and spread them out before him. Books were in Malayalam. He picked up a small book with the subtitle *Historical Research* and glanced through its contents. It appeared to me worth buying and I said,

"Prafulji, we can buy this book."

The old man took out two to three small books in English. Praful took all of them and also the book I had suggested. The bookseller was happy when Praful gave him the book at the printed price.

I said, "Will you not give us any discount?" He gave us a broad smile and said,

"Mole, rarely people buy books. Today, I'm lucky, I could sell four books. Kannan (Lord Krishna) will bless all of you."

Tina was happy looking at the old man's broad smile and flowing beard. While walking in the group, she commented,

"I never thought that he could be a bookseller. How did Alex guess it?"

Turning to Tina, Alex commented, "It is magic. I can read what's going on even in your mind right now."

"Come on! Tell me what I thought just now. If you guess it correctly, I'll bear the expense of your trip to Thiruvalla," Tina challenged.

"But anyway, you are not coming with us. Only Arjun will join me. It's my mum's ancestoral home where I can't take a girl," Alex warned.

"OK, okay, I'm not coming with you. But tell me what was in my mind?"Tina insisted.

"It is temple premises and the clever Kannan sits here. You have to be honest and tell us the truth. If my mind reading is correct, you will give us Rs. 500 and we will use it for the fuel to Thiruvalla. We are luring Achachan to get the Maruti and Lazar to drive us," Alex said.

"OK, agreed. I'll give you Rs. 500/- if you're reading is correct."

Alex came close to Tina and looked deep into her eyes. He turned towards the assembly hall, looked at the clouds above and whispered,

"It's the best place for getting married. If our friends and relatives were here, it would have been a wonderful occasion."

Tina buried her face in both her hands and virtually sat on the ground. Arjun took out her shoulder bag and searched for her wallet. She immediately got up and snatched the same from Arjun.

"It's okay. You are right. But I'll not give the money."

Before she could complete what she was saying, all cried out in a chorus,

"Oh, that's bad."

Praful came for a compromise.

"Let us get into a settlement. She dreamed of Arjun. Therefore, they can share 50–50."

Arjun was too clever. He agreed, pulled out his wallet and took out Rs. 250. Reluctantly, Tinatoo joined and gave Rs. 500 with the hope of getting the remaining Rs. 250. Alex snached away the Rs. 500 currency note and showed a thumbs-up sign to Arjun. The whole episode appeared to be pre-planned by the two to drain poor Tina. Lazar, pappa's driver, might have already tipped off these nuts about the beer parlors on the way to Thiruvalla, I thought.

Both Alex and Arjun were a few steps ahead of us. Alex's hand was on Arjun's shoulder, and both of them were whispering and giggling. Tina was unable to tolerate the scene. She looked around for some objects to throw at them. Sadly, it was temple premises; so, she couldn't get any and she hit her head, cursing her fate.

We had a close *dharsan* of Parthasarathi (Lord Krishna) and also bought a small quantity of Ambalapuzha *palpayasam* (milk porridge), which has been well known for its unique taste for centuries. Praful noted down his observations, and we reached the place where Achachan was sitting. There was enough room for all of us. A few local people sat near Achachan and they were discussing issues related to the new admissions in a local college, where he was a board member. The sprawling temple complex and the mightly antique structures opened the rich past before us. Like a flashback on a silver screen, I could visualize it as a seat of learning and empowerment during a long period, a lull on the system, the emergence of new feudal sociopolitical systems, a switchover to idol worship, introduction of mythology to suppress the majority, imposition of a variety of customs, laws and regulations to ward off the majority from the newly designed wealth-creating centers, their institutionalization process, subsequent reformation and the present status.

***

Achachan was in a corner seat, and therefore, we could take our seats on both sides of him. Praful showed him the books. He had a glance of them and said,

"These books will be helpful to understand the immediate past. A larger part of the history is forgotten or deliberately hidden, maybe due to constraints. Realize such limitations and use multidisciplinary and interagency approaches to probe into the larger part of the hidden subject."

Returning the books Achachan added,

"Let us initiate a school-of-thinking process to unearth our own strengths. There should not be any interpersonal, intercaste or interreligion conflicts related to addressing realistic studies. The strengths among us and our belief in various faiths such as Buddhism, Sikhism, Christianity, Islam and Brahmanism are drawn from our own soil. All religions address human welfare. The studies should trace out our strengths and get themselves internalized for collective empowerment."

"Sir, we would like to hear from you about the temple, its neighborhood?" Praful pleaded.

"My information is based on certain stories I heard. Most of them relate to the local chieftains of Chempakassery and stories connecting Purakkadu, a small princely province, and the recently escavated Buddha sculptures. Amateurs create confusion based on their self or group interest. Even the Department of Archeology is yet to trace out the importance of Onattukara and its neighborhood. There is a collective ignorance on the subject. I look forward to your team addressing the subject or atleast placing them before suitable forums that can take up scientific search."

The secretary looked at Achachan. Achachan paused and encouraged him to share his views.

"As you know, a soldier has to live in barracks. I had the opportunity to mix with soldiers from different parts of India. Irrespective of our language, faith, habits and practices, we all are linked by a common culture. I observe the same culture around this area in a more intensive form. I may be wrong in my observation. But as a soldier, I feel that my Christian and Muslim brothers represent their faith relatively better than I do. A Leftover like me is a lesser representative of the Hindu faith compared with the other two religions. We are less organized, and often I feel that we fail to contain our faith. Such views haunted me in my barrack, especially when we used to discuss subjects related to our faith. Take the case of this temple. Here, I am a Hindu. On hearing the different views of people, I become less intense in my faith and feel alienated. The behavior of the priests of our temples further weakens our links. My confusion is further confounded when I hear people like Bala's father. I'll be happy if anyone can enlighten me on the subject."

He looked at Achachan. His face revealed a confused mind. He explained,

"In the nearby area, we have historical support on the existence of a flourishing culture under Buddhism. Most of the *Pallies* and *Viharas* of that time were converted into Hindu temples. In certain places, the newly emerged temple enriched the economic status of the local people as trade and other services revolved around it. But they lost their institutional clout on universal education, freedom of expression, occupational choice, free mobility, independent thinking, creative work and even spiritual emancipation. The narrowing down process resulted in unhygienic living, slavery, widespread diseases, illiteracy, constant fear, threats and a blocking of their thinking process. The large-level misuse of scarce capital and human labor for construction of huge temples and lessure places to project their personal ego and vested group interests resulted in a blockade among the public in asset creation, skill upgradation, empowerment of the nation and defending it from enemies and natural calamities. As a result of the misrule, the worst things happened during the previous millennium. When other countries in Europe leaped ahead with the help of science and technology, our *Kutty* (petty) Rajas led the local provinces by tearing the clothes of their own women, which their ancestors had made them wear atleast 4,000 years ago. The culture that the Savarnas talked about and demonstrated through the example of Duryodhana on Droupathi was practiced by the *Kutty* Rajas and institutionalized by our own *Maharajas*. Wealth created through slavery was locked up in dark cellars in temples. It was deliberately denied for the development of the less privileged and kept away from them through the criteria of untouchabily. To guard and regulate the system, fraudulent habits and practices were internalized, genetically implanted and sustained through the fear psychosis. A vast majority of the Indians were kept in the dark by a powerful few, a microscopic minority, who taught them to believe that they would suffer due to their own wrong doings in their earlier birth."

He paused and again looked at us. We were shocked to hear the soldier. The social reengineering process that our minority friends could institutionalize over a period was the greatest success story I had ever heard.

Achachan added,

"If we carefully analyze the themes of the modern commercial films, one can see stories revealing this fraudulent nature and a hero fighting hard for survival. We enjoy the theme, but our timidity and the self-policing prevent us from undertaking such heroic defense acts in real life. The inability to react thrives among us even after sixty-eight years of independence. We can collectively call them corrupt, and even the Indian Parliament is unable to tune the system to their own liking. The urge for change is commercialized in the media; they sell their products and make money. Even in religious places, fraudulent practices and exploitation of the devotees continue. This culture, to a large extent, was missing in the *thuruth* and even in Onattukara. The urge perhaps still survives in such pockets in our subcontinent. Maybe due to the survival of a culture less known to us. Or, whether it is an illusion of an old man? You researchers should probe. This surviving culture still binds us, you and I."

The secretary was opening up and we could feel the hidden pain in him.

Alex interrupted,

"Sir, perhaps it is the first time we are listening to a soldier. Will you please elaborate?"

"Alex, on the weekend, we soldiers visit religious places near our cantonment. My Christian and Muslim friends have someone to listen to them in their churches or in their mosques. After attending Sunday Mass or Friday Prayer, our friends shared their experience with us. I have always missed such an opportunity to talk to a spiritual guide. In the temple I visited, no one owned me. When I was in difficulty, I was unable to share my problems with any one in those temples. I felt a vacuum in this regard. If I had lived 1,000 years earlier, I could have walked into a *Pally* or a Buddha *Vihara* and could have got some solace by meeting a monk or a teacher. I have missed such support throughout my life, especially during my service period."

He looked at Achachan. His face reflected an unowned or Leftovers' plight. He continued,

"If I'm in difficulty today, I'll run to sir. It's due to my personal attachment to him. But I'm hinting at a larger picture, a vaccum at the cultural and especially at the institutional level. Perhaps, all the Leftover in India may be feeling such a vacuum. I feel we are not well knit. We constitute eighty percentage of the population in the subcontinent. It creates insecurity, fear and distrust among the vast majority in the subcontinent. If it does, it will ruin us, our family, neighborhood and even the nation and its building process."

He paused and folding his hands, politely he whispered,

"Sir, I may be wrong. I am just a soldier. But I feel that our institutions fail to create a sense of belonging for the majority of us. The emergence of political parties, social forums, trade unions, resident associations and so on are inadequate for holding our people. We need to be part of a larger culture to accommodate the wide variety among us."

Praful showed high regards for the secretary for opening up his mind. He prompted,

"Irrespective of the age, we love to have handholding. Each one of us loves to be cared for. We enjoyed this better in our mother's lap. Even in our family and in the society, we aspire for such a holding. How far was AVP successful in the *thuruth* to fill the vacuum?"

"If we study the *Variyolas* (written laws) of the Naduvazhies (local rulers) during the seveneteenth and eighteenth centuries in Onattukara and its neighboring area, we can see that instead of handholding and protecting their subjects, the *Kutty* Rajas (local chiefs) enacted laws and devised methods to harass the majority of their subjects under the varna system. They created fear among their subjects. When a few of them introduced laws on dress code and the wearing of ornaments, others enacted laws to prevent their mobility, access to public roads, temples and common places. Even weavers were not allowed to wear the clothes they made. People who violated the laws were punished severely. Even educated Maharajas and those claiming to have extended blue blood behaved oddly. A queen, in the recent past, shamelessly walked with her bare breast before the British Resident and other invited guests. In Karthikapally, a local chief promulgated a law to kill the Avarna girls who fail to submit to the desires of the caste Hindus. Another funny *Kutty* Raja was very particular to have a state's right on the first night of the Channar girls. He insisted that the right for celebration during the first night is his royal prerogative and if he was busy, he nominated another Savarna on his behalf. And if the girl was beautiful, he himself took the trouble. Yet another guy, unable to find revenue resource, taxed his subjects' breasts. He was incapable of sourcing alternate revenue resources. The royal culture reflected third-rate hooliganism when a large part of the world was in the process of industrial revolution, commercialization and cultural integration. Even today, a microscopic minority who inherited the gene curses the missing opportunity and erects the statues of those ignorent idiots and their erotic Devans on the streets of the states' capital as a tribute to that golden era in the past."

Achachan looked at Alex and asked,

"Do you see television channels such as National Geographic, Discovery and Animal Planet?"

Alex nodded and said,

"Achachan, there is scope for reenacting the wild nature of ours through a new television channel. Lions hunt, hyenas snatch, vultures peck off the last piece of meat and the bacteria help in decomposition. The local *naduvazhies*, perhaps, returned to their own primitive culture, forgetting the lessons of the great teachers."

"Yes, that is what happened. In such a context, AVP behaved differently. I'll explain to you a few of the major incidents related to the forceful breaking of the *chattavariyola* that prevailed in this area. Tipu Sulthan was far better civilized when compared with the school of *naduvazhies* in Travancore, Cochin and Malabar during his invasion. When the fear created by him waned out, our *Kutty* Rajas and even the kings once again misbehaved. Perhaps AVP realized the advantages in creating fear among the petty law imposers of Onattukara." Achachan shared his suppressed feelings. A few more temple visitors and neighborhood friends of Achachan and the secretary added to the group of listeners. They were curious about the Delhi group and the subjects they discussed.

⁂

"Sir, we have heard about the dress code. Can you please share with us the practices that prevailed during AVP's time?" Praful asked.

Achachan smiled and looked at Tina and me.

"I don't think that our predecessors didn't wear any clothes. It's all absurd. In India, people started wearing clothes at least 4,000 years earlier. If they didn't, how come our own gods are dressed in Kancheepuram sarees in our sculptures and paintings? Even Lord Buddha and his disciples were properly dressed. A few of them even wore fashionable caps, shoes and carried walking sticks and attractive shoulder bags. Our handloom products and the imported Chinese silk were in abundance in our country. We had a well-spread settlement of handloom weavers in each cluster of villages in the Indian subcontinent. Then how can our people move naked or half naked? When Brahmanism lost its grounds, a few hooligans bribed the illiterate, fancily dressed imported priestly class and sidelined the remaining Namboothiris. They imported the new 'Brahmin' from Tamil Nadu and other neighboring states based on need. In Kerala, we have favorable climate for sex throughout the year. In north India, especially during May and June when the summer is extreme and in December and January during severe winter, it is not condusive for normal sex. The ignorant and poor imported Brahmins and the goondas who were upgraded to Kshathriyas in the *Kuttirajyams* (small provinces) couldn't think of things other other than sex for enjoyment. They framed petty laws to satisfy their urge. Their henchmen imposed them; similar to Mumbai's underworld, dons rule through their hitmen. If a good police officer is around, these goons will keep their tail in between their legs and run for their life. The same might have happened during AVP's presence, especially in the *thuruth* and its neighborhood."

He paused and looked at Alex, who was capable of imagining the run. Achachan continued,

"In the earlier days, the local weekly or biweekly markets were one of the assembly places for the people to meet and buy essentials. It was also a place for gossip, sharing food as well as for entertainment. Generally, people dress up nicely and go to such markets and fairs. It's also a place to show off, like the present malls where Alex and company do window shopping, enjoy the AC, especially during the summer in Delhi."

Achachan smiled, looked at us and he continued,

"Alex and Arjun will never agree that they visited the malls in INA, Sarojini Nagar and R. K. Puram areas nearer to JNU. And girls like Tina and Chippy will never agree that they had dressed in their best and moved around Palika Bazzar before their exams."

Achachan looked at us again with his mischievous smile and CIA vision. He tried to trace out our invasion to Palika Bazzar and the nearby Metro Cinema and the Punjabi Dhabas.

"So the girls and ladies of AVP's time also moved freely in the bazaar dressed in all kinds of fabrics such as *rowka, blouse, chatta with skirts, dhothies, mundu and narieth*, which were the popular costumes at those times. If they failed to wear clothes, how did those weavers survive? Could the Naduvazhies buy the entire clothes that those weavers made? It isn't possible. But a few miscreants, especially the Savarnas, tried to forcefully remove the clothes of a few attractive girls. They thought themselves powerful enough to unhook or untie the rowkas, as the present eveteasers do. In Arattupuzha, especially in the *thuruth*, we had a different culture. Thus, AVP was unable to tolerate the miscreants. Once, he and his men were moving on horseback in a local market near Kayamkulam. He was shocked to see a larger number of elderly ladies moving in the market without wearing upper garments. He also learned that most of these ladies were Avarnas and marginalized. In certain pockets, mentally sick hooligans dominated and they harassed women wearing upper garments. The Savarna rulers used this as a fear-generating tool for continuation of slavery, which was officially banned. During the time of AVP, rapid changes were going on. In many pockets organized efforts were made by Christian missionaries and Islamic leadership for checking the malpractices. The British government kept away from any interference in the internal affairs of the local rajas, as they wanted their support for colonialization."

He paused and looked at Praful, who was scribbling in his book. Achachan continued,

"Why did AVP raise his voice against such atrocities? This is a subject for detailed study. One of my elders told me that one day he witnessed a couple of hooligans tearing the blouse of a beautiful girl in the market at Kayamkulam. He interfered and could physically stop it. However, the incident disturbed his mind. He asked his men to buy all the available *thorthu* (a light towel made by handloom weavers) in the market and to supply them to the women not having upper garments. Standing in the market, he distributed more than a thousand *thorthu* and asked them to wear the same as upper garments. In case of any problem, he also offered them protection. It was said that AVP and his trusted men made surprise visits to ensure a better culture: the culture we lost, due to the misrule."

"Was there any hesitation from the women to wear upper garments in those days?"Tina asked.

"Yes, there was a certain hesitation. It might have happened due to the habit. Similar to men, women too might have loved to wear a small piece of cloth around their waists and work in humid climate. If there was a winter season in Kerala, our *Kutty* Rajas and even *Maharajas* would never have thought about framing such stupid laws. Rather, many of them were ignorant about the very existence of winter and extreme summer in the northern part of our country."

"Can it be a cleverly introduced tool to marginalize the Leftover, create fear among them, thereby ensuring the supremacy of Savarnas?" I asked.

"The motive definitely was malicious. Those were not fit for a ruler or a *Naduvazhi*. It tells volumes of their barbarian culture. Leaders such as AVP were led by the true Indian culture. Unfortunately, even after sixty-eight years of independence, we are only in the process of change. The bad culture still persists among us. It needs a thorough reengineering process for cultural improvement. In free India, we are still settling down, with the mindset of a traveller in a reserved compartment of the Indian Railways, who is on a long journey. Within the past sixty-eight years, we failed to address our basic cultural issues. Our spiritual leaders also couldn't address them from a larger perspective. As a result, there occured larger drifts; interregional, intergroup and even interpersonal cultural conflicts, resulting in an unusual unrest. Today, we are less satisfied. We feel less secure. We also miss the mutual trust and care. There is abject poverty in expressing love, care and compassion. Recently, a young mother told me that she is unable to reciprocate love to her own children. There is a growing miser's feeling in expressing ourselves and our emotions. It is like being censored at all levels. The missing culture appears to be the major culprit. Perhaps AVP had a dominant cultural chemistry that we presently aspire for," Achachan said.

"Did we lose those cultural qualities due to centuries of misrule?" Alex asked.

"If we feel that something is really missing among us, we need to find out what it is. Why are parents thrown out of their own home when they become incapable? Why are a large number of families broken? Why is there a lack of trust among politicians, bureaucrats and the public? Perhaps, such things happen due to the missing links; which need probing," Praful said.

"If we study these situations carefully, we might be able to arrive at their solutions too," he added.

"Sir, empowerment of our women is one of the important subjects that we talk about in an attempt to address and to bring in the desired changes. During the time of AVP, did such subjects catch his attention?"

"Can I share a few facts?" Looking at Achachen, the secretary intervened,

"In the *thuruth*, both boys and girls were encouraged to attend Asan School. A few of the girls also learned Kalari through the help of the *Kalari Asan* who visited certain localities.

It was AVP who personally encouraged participation of girls and women in all possible activities. The network of women for making quality dry fish through regular collection of fish, their sun drying, further sorting, grading and packaging for bulk sale gave way to the success story of female participation in the *thuruth*. The system subsequently was adapted by the coir processors and traders in Alappuzha district. In fact, AVP also encouraged women to inculcate the habit of saving money and buying gold ornaments during Onam. It is said that women who were associated with fish drying and marketing were able to purchase gold ornaments such as earrings and studs, bangles and often a necklace. A goldsmith called Krishnan *Thattan* (goldsmith) and a couple of his coworkers used to move with AVP for meeting such demands made by poor women. During his time, in *Kizhakekara* (eastern river bank), Avarna women were more enthusiastic to wear gold ornaments that were denied by the local rulers. In certain places, the Savarna's goons forcefully took away even the earrings and nose rings, hurting and tearing their bodies. Near the present Chavara Sankaramangalam, a place very near to our *thuruth*, the ladies were afraid of wearing nose rings, which they thought was only the prerogative of Savarna women. Then, AVP made 1,000 gold *Mukoothies* (small nose wear) and Krishnan Thattan; for fourteen long days, his men perched their tents at Sankaramangalam and put the nose rings on long-awaiting women. It was an extended celebration, and AVP met the entire cost. It is often heard that even elderly ladies waited for long hours with small reflectors to see their faces lit up with a golden *mukuthy*, a lifelong desire that was finally fulfilled. The process really empowered the women to come out in large groups and in breaking the prevalent Kutty Rajas" laws and customs."

The secretary was interrupted by Achachan, and he said,

"This process of women empowerment perhaps resulted in awakening their own long-felt genetic upgradation. If we study the achievement of women in Onattukara, one can observe that they had come forward and taken up challenging roles and responsibilities in the field of economic production, performing arts, health care, judiciary and social work. Even today, there is a larger visibility of the ladies from Onattukara in almost all walks of life in Kerala and especially in visual media such as films and television." The secretary paused.

Praful was scribbling on his writing pad, and Achachan added,

"A good number of drama groups, artistes well known in the field of *kathaprasangam* (storytelling), drama and *Kathakali,* world-famous writers such as Thakazhi Sivasankara Pillai, filmmaker Padmarajan and many of the young Malayalam film celebrities, as well as committed politicians with outstanding talents hail from this place. We have a talented female politician from Alappuzha who is of my age and is still active. During her youth, she joined the Communist Party and contributed to the party and the government like any of the performing male leaders. She belonged to the stamped Avarna community. But her intellectual capability in steering the state was proved as early as 1957."

Tina intervened and asked Praful,

"Sir, can we suggest a subject related to women empowerment in Onattukara for any of our M Phil students for dissertation?"

"Why not? You can develop a synopsis, convince your research guide and, subsequently, seek the approval of the research committee," Praful advised.

"Chippy was telling me that a lady here chopped off her breast to protest against the system of collecting tax on breasts. It is the daredevil attitude of a lady to stop such a corrupt practice. Such incidents are lesser known to people outside Kerala. As you know, I'm from Malkangari, a tribal district in Orissa. You all know that Buddhism was butchered in Orissa and we tribals are the Leftover large segment that is still cut away from the mainstream of life for more than eight centuries. Now people call us primitive, docile, illiterate, poor and look to us as a liability to the nation. But no one speaks about the Dark Age and the atrocities we were subjected to."

Tina was gasping for breath; Achachan's chortle reverberated and the small crowd around us baffled.

"I hear the roaring of a lioness of Malkangiri. The people of Malkangiri were in the dark; perhaps, you should hold the lamp lit by a hero like AVP. Make it a larger fire and show them the light. The Buddhists in the whole world will support you in the process of resurrection. Even all religions in the world will support you, because their roots are one and the same. The teachings of Buddha, Jesus Christ, Prophet Muhammed Nabi and Guru Nanak are one and the same. These religions have their roots in the great masters who teach on truth, love and compassion. Therefore, there is no difference among us. For empowerment, we need local leadership. By our luck, we had AVP at a time of our urgent need. The culture has to survive, resurrect and spread throughout the subcontinent. Fortunately, we have inherited relatively better-refined genes through the teachings of Buddhism. During the Dark Period, obviously these suffered quality degradation. However, with larger efforts, we can rejuvenate them. Ritually, we celebrate Enlightenment Day as Diwali without internalizing its values. Through various myths and stories, the vested interests could keep us, the large majority, in the dark even on Diwali day. Both Mugal and colonial rulers used the same tool to capture political power. Even after Indian independence, the new leadership also wore the same fur for convenience. Currently, in the new sociopolitical and globalization scenario, we don"t get time and the desired will to address such an important subject. As a result, the majority of us are still left out. They feel they are yet to be included in the nation-building process. By showing dolls, those who are in power capture votes. It is ritually celebrated once in every five years."

Achachan paused, asked Tina to come nearer and stroked her head. Tina curled up nearer to his knees and felt the comfort of his great care.The crowd was moved by his words. Arjun used his handkerchief so that he could hide his wet eyes, guarding his masculine qualities in front of Tina.

Alex said, "These are the missing link of love, truth and compassion. Many of our leaders often remind us of the subject. In fact, AVP practiced them. He could warm up the *thuruth* and the nearby area. Somehow, we poured cold water on such an inherent trait of ours. Then, people like Achachen and his group attempted to keep such traits alive. They are igniting our own culture. It sparkles compassion, care and love. In Sri Lanka, we have been missing it for the past thirty years due to our own ignorance. We, brothers, fought and none of us could win. We lost precious time during globalization. As a result, our present generation is weak and less competent, except for perhaps our cricket team."

He looked at Achachan and the secretary and continued,

"From the war, we realized the extent of damage that a small group of us can do to protect their vested interests. In India, with the help of a few, they massacred the learned, captured public empowerment centers such as *Pally, Viharas* and convents, physically destroyed the culture of the village economy, the *pathikrama* and destroyed the very concept of *tharavad.* Sir, I learned that we shall be visiting the nearby place Karimady to see the idol of Lord Buddha that has been recovered from the nearby paddy field. Why are we reduced to that kind of a cultural degradation? We should make collective efforts to unearth the role played by people like AVP in the Indian subcontinent. My roots in Thiruvalla and Sri Lanka enable me to be responsible to address this subject as a researcher. Through collective effort, we can learn about our rich past and this knowledge will help each one of us in strengthening ourselves and our neighborhood. Thus, AVP can be one of the role models in the learning processes."

Alex paused and looked at Achachan.

Achachan smiled and said,

"Karimady is nearby and it is a five-minute drive from here. Nearer to the monument that is currently preserved by the Department of Archeology, you will find two beautiful ancient structures. You may observe their utility and also their nearness to the river. Based on your skill in research, you will be able to learn many things. This temple at Ambalapuzha, the structures at Karimady, Cherthala, Harippad, Oachira and Thrikkunnapuzha will lead you to Sreemoolavasam and its cultural link with Sabarimala. The locations of these shrines have to be studied by using Vasthu Sasthra and their approach by road and also by water transport. With the support of science and technology, its connectivity during the earlier period can be traced. Somehow, we have a fear that the truth will weaken us. I don't think so. We are all Indians. Along with the times, we have also changed. Perhaps the time is right for further changes. The changes are required for the vast majority of the Leftover. Without their empowerment and active participation, India can never achieve the status of a developed economy. Land allocation, reservation in government jobs and subsidies are only temporary solutions. We should make them know their own past status, and the process will build confidence among them. The great Indian shyness is due to the larger fear in their gene. We should make them fearless, as Rabindranath Tagore had told us a century ago. In sports, we often talk about our missing killer instinct. When our leaders themselves forget the sportsman's spirit, how can we attain the collective killer instinct?"

Achachan took the help of Tina to get up from the most beautiful place in the temple. He slowly walked to the temple gate. This pond and its steps perhaps know the truth they have witnessed the testing times. With careful steps, I got down from the *melkettu*, more confused than what I was earlier. With bowed head, I joined the group in search of the *Kuttan* (mischievous kid) at Karumady.

To me, Karimady looked like a large seat of learning. Why the local people fail to showcase such a treasure to the world, I wondered! In between the two temples, on the left and right, Karimadikuttan sits and smiles at the past 600 years of unfriendly changes in Onattukara and the neighboring places. A couple of farmers joined us on seeing Achachan. They together moved to the Kavil Kamaroopam Bhadrakali Kshethram and sat on the raised platform. We moved to pay our humble respect to the

Great Teacher. A signboard of the Department of Archeology read, "Protected Monument—Karimadikuttan—AD 10th Century Carved-Out Sculpture—District Collector." The tiny structure was poorly kept, as if commenting on the present status of Buddhism and the Leftover people in India. We all looked at the great surviving Kuttan of Karumady. He was charcoal black, young, energetic, friendly and mischievous looking. A great shame brewed up in me. I looked at the others. All looked dejected. Our heads hung in shame. Alex used his camera and he clicked many snaps of the area, which was less than 200 square feet. Praful removed his shoes, went close to the sculpture and observed its features. He is one of the brilliant researchers of Delhi University, a world-class scholar in his scientific studies in the past.

Praful whispered to Alex,

"Can we have a few close-up snaps of the sculpture from different angles?"

He stepped out of the platform and Alex took a few snaps. He zoomed his lens. The sun gave him full bright light, casting no shadows on the Great Teacher.

There was an unusual silence among us. Each one of us might have been thinking of the circumstances that led us to commit the greatest crime on earth, crushing our own most reverend teacher for centuries in mud. There is a great curse on us, the curse on the wrongdoers, and the killers of a great culture. The smarter had cleverly addressed the larger public as, "Brahmana Sapam" (the curse of Brahmins). Obviously, it is the great curse that we all once bured in our subconscious mind and the Savarnas cleverly marketed it in their favor for physical gains. It was also a clever social reengineering. Of late, the stamped and the Leftover, the larger set of people in the subcontinent, have been slowly learning to come out of the millennium-old trap. One can never keep everything in the dark all the time, I felt.

We sat with Achachan and the secretary on the temple platform. Alex, Praful and Arjun moved to the nearby temple currently called "Sree Sankara Narayana Moorthy Kshetram."

"It's a strange place with unusual topography and it is equally unusual for the two temples to be nearer to each other. They need not be temples. They may be schools of different thoughts or separate accommodation for scholars, male and female," Tina looked at Achachan and said. Both of them smiled.

"We are just guides. You have to be serious and find out what exactly they were in that period and for what purpose time had used them. And why the sculptures of Lord Buddha were thrown out and stamped in the mud?" The secretary watched Tina with probing eyes.

"In Orissa, we have hundreds of places where such incidents took place. Perhaps in the whole of India, thousands of such places might be available for conducting in-depth studies." She looked disturbed and took extra efforts to hide her feelings.

Achachan smiled and said,

"In Orissa, you have many such incidents. Majority of the people in Orissa are marginalized and live in poverty and superstition. The power-wielding minority presently stamp them as tribal, scheduled caste, other backward caste and so forth. They were kept away from the socioeconomic and spiritual centers. By missing two generations, that is, sixty years, you become a barbarian or a primitive. If a set of people are kept away from the mainstream of life for 800 long years, how can they be smart and fit enough to join the globalization process?"

He looked at Tina, a potential change agent of the Leftover in Orissa, I guessed. Achachan has skills to identify promising youth for the rebuilding process.

The boys also joined us. They were gloomy and sat nearer to the secretary.

"Now what?" the secretary asked.

"It looks very sad and unfortunate to know about such a Dark Period even in the southern most tip of the subcontinent. This state could climb and achieve the highest Human Development Index (HDI) matching with that of the developed countries within six decades after independence. Their genes might have undergone a long-term upgradation process as a result of its close association with gurus, social change agents and handholders in an early social system. With the availability of the new social order during the mid-twenties, they again sprung to their original status. Perhaps these two structures may be the earlier empowerment centers of the local area for men and women where the earlier teachers taught, relaxed and handheld the local people," Praful said.

"There is nothing to worry about. There are better hopes for the younger generation," Achachan pacified us.

He stood up and took a seat near Praful, kept his hand on his shoulder and said,

"The reasons for the higher HDI are not due to our politicians, administrators or the *Kutty* Rajas. But they are due to the huge efforts of our loving *Asans* (the village teachers) and the Buddhist monks and scholars who taught us about better hygiene, healthy food habits, widespread practices of the *Ayurveda Vaidyas*, the system of body massage during the monsoon, the scientific advantage of keeping *Kavu* and *Kulam* near our habitats, the harvesting of rainwater, the preservation of waterbodies, the development of large herbatoriums, the maintenance of hills and forests through staying within the forest during old age with wild animals, insects and varied flora and fauna. Presently, politicians and a few bureaucrats claim the credit for Kerala's high literacy, health and hygiene. But why do leaders and officers of equal authority fail to achieve this in other states? They are unable to answer. Or, let us post our most efficient officers in other places where there is a shortage of them and give them an opportunity to prove their mettle."

Tina felt comfortable with Achachan and she asked,

"Achachan is there any relation between the presence of Buddhist monks in our forests and the large number of people who were driven out from their Pathikramas, towns and villages and who took shelter in the forest area?"

"You raised a valid question. You are smart to relate to certain unfortunate things that happened in our past. If an economic blockade is imposed for centuries, will it not lead to an underdeveloped status? Given an opportunity, can a girl from Malkamgiri get admission in JNU on merit and raise such a wonderful question? This reflects our brilliance. The hidden genetic quality spurts out at the very first opportunity."

Achachan smiled at Tina. She turned her face away to hide her tears. Her sobbing sound broke the silence of the temple. I got up, went near her and held her close to me. The villagers were confused. But they could realize why their daughter was in tears. Something bad had happened to all of us, they felt. I could hear the wailing of the Leftover through her.

"It's not the time to weep. It's the time to muster courage and enlighten the Leftover to our rich past and to assign leadership for rebuilding the nation. Let us make them aware that they are the loving sons and daughters of the Greatest Teacher on earth; all of us have stood by His ideals for centuries and we are His loving children. Your efforts will recharge the body cells of the Leftover and ignite the genetic excellence subdued for centuries. And, like you Tina, they will also perform their best and the transformation will brighten the subcontinent."

Achachan once again called Tina to his side. Like the birds that are sheltered in the shadow of a banyan tree, she went close to him and clung to him.

Looking at his scribbling pad, Praful tried to read out something. He said,

"Sir, the names of the two temples, Kavil Kamapuram Sree Bhadrakali Kshethram and Sree Narayana Moorthy Shkethram appear odd to me. Whether it is due to my own limitation in understanding it, I doubt?"

Achachan burst into laughter. The secretary also struggled to suppress his own titter. Achachan clarified,

"For what purpose did a set of our own people create fear, even in such empowerment centers? How does the looters' culture intrude into such places along with idol workship? Why did the clout of Himsa get institutionalized in such beautiful spots? What is required more for the people? A place for butchering them or a place for formulating socially useful programs and projects? You researchers have to unearth these. We are ordinary people and have limitations in analyzing the pros and cons of history."

Achachan paused and again he giggled. The villagers joined, perhaps without understanding the seriousness of the subject.

"The bad words used in the military and police force may be due to the recently inherited culture. During peace time, we soldiers are treated as enemies by the majority of our superiors. Only a minority of them have the faculty to identify that their true enemies are elsewhere. The *Kutty* Rajas here too had the same culture. Perhaps, even today, in an elected government, we treat the opposition as our enemy and slowly the ruling party treats the whole public as their enemy. This makes them sit in opposition after the next election. Commercial television channels sell them as the Great Indian Circus or Poli-tricks. Stimulating the body is easy, but an inner stimulation takes time. Like the British who have changed Kozhikode to Calicut, Kollam to Quilon, for their convenience and to appease their own group, our predecessors might have changed the names of these temples during the sixteenth and eighteenth centuries, when the takeover process under Brahmanism was at its peak in Kerala and was led by the *Kutty* Rajas, the upgraded goondas, *Madampies* (feudal lords), *Naduvazhikal* (local chiefs), Rajas and Maharajas. Like the present deemed universities awarding graduation, postgraduation and doctoral status, earlier Savarnaguilds awarded a new social status based on their well-laid norms and the money they received. The process of grabbing the existing institutions and renaming them to suit their mission were usual practices under the process of change."

Achachan paused, looked into the eyes of Praful and said,

"As you have rightly felt, the names are not apt for these structures and presently they serve no purpose. We have to find the missing names and trace out their real utility. With timely changes required, we have to make them alive. We have to address this reengineering process in all similer pockets wthin the subcontinent. It will open up new avenues for the large majority of the Leftover to participate and to contribute to the nation-building process. Presently, a large number of the performers among us are alienated, and a few of them are armed. Their discontent can lead to prolonged civil wars, as happened in Sri Lanka. So far, we have been able to avoid such situations while incurring large hidden costs. We should collectively realize the subjects, and our national policies shoud be more accommodative to absorb the aspirations of the rising Leftover, the sizable majority in the Indian Union. I feel that the youth will play a major role in the process of emerging change."

Arjun was standing facing us. He added,

"In Orissa, the process appears to be too large. In thousands of places, we may have to carefully and collectively readdress."

"Yes, the Leftover there constitute more than ninenty percentage of the population. But in Kerala, forty percentage of her population has already embraced new faith and their status on development is relatively better visible."

Tina had a direct talk with Arjun while the others watched.

"It will take a couple of centuries for the Leftover in Orissa to realize the subject."

Arjun shared his concern.

"Reaching the world is faster at present. Perhaps, through the present communication system and electronic media, the need for a cultural change process will reach and also stimulate them in a shorter time,"

Tina said and her voice was optimistic.

The group was nearer to the larger subject, I felt.

Encouraging the youth, Achachan consolidated,

"Where there is a will, there is a way. Here, no one will become a loser. Certain myths and our false egos only will vanish. But this will strengthen the confidence-building process in each local area in our country. Through a handshake, we all will win. By forgiving and accommodating each other, we will be able to internalize the teachings of our gurus. Our places of worship will undergo timely transformations and will become empowerment centers on spiritual, social and overall development. The establishment of new development centers with local participation will make all of us participate in the globalization process. It will enable us to indulge in better and productive utilization of the locally available natural and human resources for improving the quality of the entire life system. Still, we have with us the inbred gene of not allowing others to work, especially the strong clip the wings of the weak. A bad culture unfortunately got internalized. It needs to be changed."

Achachan paused and smilingly added,

"Why do you scholars have to probe the use of words such as *Kamaroopa* in a place of worship?"

Vakil interrupted,

"We should internalize the merits of each religion and we should use their infrastructure for collective socioeconomic development and welfare. Building a secular nation was the dream of our national leaders. For this, we have to leave aside specific rigidities related to our religion and caste. And you youth can achieve it. In each village, we should build, nurse and develop such culture. The elected grama panchayat, their skills and their development funds should be used for the revival and rebuilding process in the local area. Through the process, we can revive our own missing culture and regain confidence."

I looked at vakil, our president. He smiled at me.

The group decided to proceed to Haripad and to visit Sree Subrahmania Swami Maha Kshethram and the nearby Mannarassala, two surviving institutions under the extinct larger Sreemoolavasam cultural hold. It was 11:30 in the morning, and we decided to make use of the presence of Achachan and the secretary. By lunchtime, Achachan would return to Mangalam.

***

During the drive, Praful referred his notes and referring to a point, he said,

"Achachan, we heard about Oachira and Mannarassala. Each one has its own identity. We like to hear more about these shrines. It may help us to make firm our views on comparable shrines elsewhere in the country."

Achachan turned towards us, smiled and said,

"We also heard many cock and bull stories on Oachira and Mannarasala during our lifetime. My advice to your team is that these centers appeared to us as major empowerment pockets in the past. But between the sixteenth and eighteenth centuries, our loving *Kutty* Rajas made certain make-shift arrangements for introducing the new social order for their own survival. However, those were temporary in nature. The present generation can well understand those fallacious changes. If those changes were useful to humanity, they will sustain and attract world attention. Otherwise, they will slowly be reduced to meaningless entertainment or *Peykoothu,* as said in Malayalam."

Achachan paused, looked at the secretary and continued,

"I have heard you sharing your views on the Shreemoolavasam lost culture with temple visitors. Why can't you share your views with these people?"

The secretary smiled and obliged,

"The concept of *Kavu* and *Kulam* (small pocket of dense vegetative cover with a water pond nearby) predominates in both the places. It may be places where earlier teachers or scholars used to take a break during their long journey. In those days, they might have travelled mostly by foot. Therefore, there was a need for getting relaxed and refreshed. Often, a few might have loved to meditate and a few also engaged in creativity in their respective fields of specialization. Many might have shared their skills and knowledge for the benefit of the local people and also handheld the local administration to address timely required welfare and the process of change. The process enabled them to retain the knowledge and skills on science, technology, family, social and spiritual empowerment and their transfer to the vast majority of the common people. Access to knowledge and skills was not denied to any one in the Indian subcontinent at that time. This process enabled the community to modernize agriculture, agro-processing, handloom, and handicraft. It helped in widening their trade, technology transfer, universal literacy and developing skills in martial arts for self-defense. It further enabled better hygiene and social living in the communes, development of Ayurveda, *Marmavidya*, body rejuvenation, development of various art forms, local markets, development of surface and water transport, annual celebrations in temples called *Uthsavams* and making the larger gathering of people to meet, exchange their views, build relations, sell their products and skill for collective empowerment. If you visit and study the various heritage centers in Kerala, you can trace out from the existing structures and the sorrounding geographical features that a collective institutionalization process survived in such pockets for more than a millennium."

The secretary paused, looked at each one of us and continued,

"It is scientifically proved that a thick vegetative cover can attract rain and recharge the groundwater. As water is the most essential item for survival, those monks might have encouraged the development of *Kavu* and *Kulam*. Ahimsa practiced by the monks, over a long period, might have strengthened a culture of coexistence of animals, reptiles, birds and insects in such places. A practice of lighting an oil lamp for reading or reciting after sunset and feeding the animals might have been initiated by the monks. When they left the place for their further travel, the local people might have continued the practice of lighting the oil lamp and feeding the reptiles, animals and birds. And the practice might have got institutionalized. Mannarasala may reflect the larger devotion of a family and their love in preserving the mighty culture left by our loving teachers."

There was a silence and Alex broke the same. He said,

"We have presently the Self Help Groups (SHGs), Joint Liability Groups (JLGs), Cooperative Societies, Artisans' Guilds, Farmers' Clubs and various other clubs of the youth, ladies, for the elites, for retired people, trade union forums, resident associations, spiritual groups, groups for entertainment and fans' associations. Can we think of an institutional setup in those days around the *Kavu* and *Kulam*?"

"Definitely yes," Achachan said. He looked at us and added,

"Absence of quality leadership is one of the limiting factors in our current social life. As a result, our sociopolitical and cultural forums often become too narrow and selfish. This leads to a suboptimum level of performance, corruption, dissatisfaction and the tragic death of such institutions. Inspite of the changes in leadership, through periodical elections, nominations or deputation, the system fails to bring desired results. I feel that the incompetency of our leaders is the major cause for the poor performance. Even the government-supported empowerment programs in Kerala are unable to achieve their goals due to the missing skills in leadership and inadequate organizational talents. Inspite of the regular involvement of the senior officials, regular training programs to upgrade the skills and productivity, we remain poor in our productive efficiency, as well as in the quality of our products and services. This reflects our own collective incapability. If we had nursed those old schools right from the Asan schools at the village level to the world-class universities at Nalanda and Thakshasila over a period of a thousand years, our country and our people could have marched well ahead. Now, we rely more on borrowed ideologies, science and technology. When they reach us, they become obsolete. The culture that is imposed on us never allows us to be liberalized. The manufacturing sectors in the Indian economy for first fifty years continued to be the privilege of the vested interests. Under the licence raj, entrepreneurs' freedom was curtailed by our own democratically elected governments. Even after independence, we continue to be slaves in most of the fields, including politics, science and technology and even in sports and games. Our mindset on slavery makes us shy and submissive, and the so-called privileged class continues to misrule. The newly gained freedom is used mostly by their near and dear. They do not allow others to perform. This culture is celebrated to express power, social status and to make money. The administration draws ecstasy in replicating the culture. They are the flag bearers of the emerging culture. Our gene could inherit more from our immediate painful past. A deliberate stimulation to delve deep into our own rich past is a larger social reengineering. Only people such as AVP can attempt it. Now, it is our turn. I look towards youth like you with hope. Presently, the majority are used by them as watchdogs. In Travancore, Maravas were used to butcher the common man by a minority offering social status such as Kshathriyahood at a heavy price. The same practice often continues with a pouch of illicit brew, a packet of parattas and fried chicken."

Achachan paused and waited. We all were in a mood to listen him. He continued,

"We, the Leftover should realize our own status and unconditionally accept and acknowledge the performers, irrespective of their religion, caste and creed. In India, we are yet to realize our great past, the missing links that can connect us together. The centers of learning created during the Buddhist period were destroyed by a few vested interests among us. By careful introduction of untouchability, a variety of mythology-based gods, customs, practices, superstitions, black magic, bloodshed and prostitution, they could create fear and suppress the majority as slaves for a few centuries. They destroyed the earlier empowerment centers throughout the subcontinent. In Kerala, the process started centuries late and it is our luck that even today, in a few places, the rich culture can be traced out. You may still find meditation centers, libraries, playgrounds, *kalaries*, *Asan* schools and even remains of the ancient *Chaithyas, Kalithattu, Pattambalam*, *Kavu* and *Kulam*, in many of the public places near the present temples. Similarly, we can also locate a few *Kavu* and *Kulam* that are still preserved even in the midst of the cities in Kerala. Many living around such places may not know the importance of those sites. But an unknown attachement to them leads them to protect such places. Can we say it is a genetic inheritance of the rich past?" he paused.

"I think both Christianity and Islam missed out on the advantages of having *Kavu* and *Kulam* in their places of worship," Alex noticed.

"No, churches and mosques in many places internalized it, especially those earlier established by the resource people. But when the present generation got the power, they ingnored the concepts such as *Kavu* and *Kulam*, may be due to the changes in priority, inadequate resources or their limited awareness,"

Achachan explained.

"Development of the infrastructure mentioned earlier perhaps had a relationship with the timely required knowledge for the society and the interest of the local chief. Even today, you can observe people with better creativity around the *Kavu* and *Kulam*. It is a subject that needs in-depth studies. People living around such places may have certain advantages," Achachan said.

Ajith enquired, "Shall we first visit Mannarasala and then Haripad Temple?"

We were nearing Haripad and as per Achachan's advice, we parked the car first at Mannarasala. All of us kept our footwear inside the car and stepped out of the car. The air was still cool and pleasant. An unusual fragrance filled the dense forest. In their quietness, both the smell and the sand took us to a time of a great culture.

Tina, Arjun and I formed a subgroup and walked. Praful, Alex and the secretary moved as the main group. Achachan and Ajith Chettan went inside the administrative office.

The large compound was clean and well kept. People observed perfect silence befitting the place. Tina got excited, may be due to a forest such as Malkangiri and the proximity of Arjun. She said,

"Arjun, I want to roll down in the whole compound. It's so serene and beautiful!"

Arjun pointed to a tropical forest-like spot and gestured to move like Tarzan. A multilayer vegetative cover was there, helping us to recall our lost memories. Under the huge trees, the smaller ones were well protected; beneath them, bushes and grass grew. The climbers crawled happily in all possible ways and embraced each tall tree differently. Nature's variety was visible, and the chirping of birds and insects made us feel better owned by her.

The group joined in front of the temple and Alex said,

"I feel jealous of our forefathers. They used these places for creative work, meditation and social empowerment, a fabulous cost-effective idea. I think, Delhi University and JNU officials should visit such places and reintroduce them into their campus. When temperature increases in Delhi, we can't have creative thinking in those concrete jungles."

Praful smiled and intervened,

"Do you know why our gods don't wear woollen garments?"

The question took us by surprise. We tried to imagine a Hindu god wearing a woollen garment; however, we could easily spot Jesus and his disciples in that kind of a costume.

Arjun came forward and said,

"Perhaps, those gods were created by scholars who were not exposed to extreme winter. Or, there was no such severe winter in those days due to the thick vegetative cover in the Indian subcontinent."

"Those are serious issues and each one of us should have a mind to find the truth as a researcher. We should approach such issues with our brain and not with our emotions."

Praful cautioned us and continued,

"These are our national treasures. A family has preserved the culture for centuries and I'm grateful to them for their wisdom and commitment. I have never seen such a fabulous place in my life."

"In Sri Lanka, we have similar places even in the heart of Colombo. A few of the Buddha Viharas in Colombo too have similar *Kavu*; in a few places, we also have *Kulams* (ponds). Maybe the Kulams were lost due to urbanization."

Praful and Alex sat near a corner in front of the temple, sketched and filled in their notebooks.

"I'm seeing such a place for the first time in my life," Tina whispered.

Holding my hand, she walked and continued,

"The whole surroundings make us feel close to nature. An unusual harmony and love for coexistence are felt here. It is quite unique." I could now guess how Sreemoolavasam had flourished in those times and how a local hero such as AVP could emerge even after a millennium.

She sat down on a platform and started playing with the white sand around. She made tiny heaps of sand and placed ants over it. They slipped down and ran for their life.

"For the small creature, it's a great fall," I said.

Tina was quick to respond.

"For us too, a thousand years' slip. For nature, it's too short a period."

All of us felt equally sad at our great fall. Alex and Praful were serious and scribbled in their notepads. We sat silently. I closed my eyes and imagined how the place would have looked a thousand years ago. I could see in my mind the silent movements of the monks, the scholars and local people taking care of them and a few seriously listening. It would have been a five-star facility during those times. The needs of the people might have been simple and limited. The thin population and abundantly available food might have given them enough leisure for creative work, mutual help and enjoyment.

Ajith Chettan came and handed over a few books to Praful, maybe books on Mannarasala.

He said, "Let us move to Haripad Temple, another shrine reflecting traces of the lost Sreemoolavasam culture. It is nearby and we can reach there within a few minutes." He gave us small paper packets containing prasadam given at Mannarasala.

We all joined him. Within a few minutes, we got down from the car to see Sree Subrahmanya Swami Maha Kshethram at

Haripad. It's a large temple under Travancore Devaswam Board (a government-appointed professional body responsible for maintenance of the Hindu temples). The temple had a copper roof, and the three large *thazhikakudams* enhanced its majestic appearance. The gigantic granite lamps and thousands of oil lamps surrounding the temple walls added to the enchanted sight. The temple ponds were crystal clear, and their masonary work reflected craftsmanship. We all sat with Achachan and the secretary near a small sandalwood tree at the left side of the temple.

We looked at Achachan and he said,

"During the time of the process of change under the varna system, gods such as Shiva, Krishna, Subrahmanyan, Ganesh and Bhadrakali were installed in places of Viharas, the empowerment centers lead by Buddhists. In Buddhism itself, at a later period, a set of its followers introduced idol workship and they installed idols of Lord Buddha and his mother Tara. During the subsequent process of change, they were removed and the new idols, a set of new gods and goddesses, were installed. People who defended the shrines were killed brutally, and the followers of the Great Teacher were kept at a distance. The restrictions imposed on Avarnas on temple entry have their roots in such social hegemony. In Kerala, the whole process was delayed by a few more centuries due to the scattered living of the people and relatively better developed local provinces that were strong Buddhist seats of learning. Its cultural ties and nearness with Sri Lanka where Buddhism flourished also delayed the process of change that was brought in by a different set of power grabbers under the newly emerging feudal and centralized power structure under the Rajas/Maharajas."

He paused and looked at us for clarifications. We loved to listen and he continued.

"The Viharas, the Chaithyas and other places of common use belonged to the community. The local chiefs with the help of emerging Brahmanism were subjected to an artificial competition to get the new status on Kshathriyahood at a higher price. The process was wealth creation for Brahmins. The emerging Kshathriyas were treated as slaves by the clever clergy. With the help of the newly created breed, they killed the Buddhist monks and the people who supported them. They drove away those who sympathized with the monks. The monks had taught nonviolence for more than a millennium, and they could do only good Karmas as taught by their teachers. The most terrified took shelter in the interior forests. The relatively less scared lived on its periphery and near the villages. The brave fought and only a few survived. Conversion to other religions also took place in a phased manner. Conversion might have happened first among the surviving defenders; then, among people who lived on the periphery of the villages. In Kerala, conversion to Christianity was initiated first in coastal area, then along the riverside and, subsequently, under the foothills. With the availability of transport and better communication, conversion even took place in high ranges; and of late, among the forest dwellers."

Achachan paused and looked at us.

"But why didn't Brahmins themselves raise a single word against conversion?" Alex asked.

Achachan smiled and continued,

"Because a few Brahmins themselves were recently converted from another faith, Buddhism. The truth behind the Brahmanical change process was commercial, and it was known to the public. Subsequently, they wrote cock and bull stories, which the Leftover were unable to read because they were denied basic education and reduced to soil slaves. Even untouchability was developed to hide Brahmanical incompetencies such as the confidential papers kept by the present elected governments. If people got opportunities to mingle, they will get a chance to know them and realize their merit. With untouchability, they could keep them away. If the Brahmins were serious about untouchability (for reasons better known to them), how could they sleep with Avarna or Shudra girls? And they even tried to institutionalize the process. It was prevailing in Kerala even during the beginning of the twentieth century. Only eminent leaders such as Mannathu Padmanabhan could drive the bad culture out from the Leftover, especially in Kerala. Through constant brainwashing, Brahmins could impose such privileges and exploit a larger set of people for more than three centuries. Slowly, they realized the trap and came out of their clutches during the first quarter of the twentieth century."

Alex was again on his feet and reflected unrest through his body language. He asked,

"How they can be so cruel? Are the Brahmins invaders?"

"No, not at all; they are our own loving brothers. A few of our own people who were interested more in physical pleasure at the cost of others, cleverly made use of the peaceful canvas of coexistence of the people in small provinces under the overall guidance of Buddhism and through a great culture that we had inherited through the Vedas. The initiators might have mustered power first with the help of a few Buddhist monks and were successful in capturing a few Buddha Viharas. Slowly, they might have inducted a few musclemen to kill and suppress those who defended themselves. A few of the then existing Kalari groups and a few communities having an aptitude for criminal deeds might have joined the process. And, later, they were awarded with Kshathriyahood on payments. The whole process might have taken a few centuries for translation. But the majority was against the process. Unfortunately, under Chathur Varna, entire Avarnas became hostile. It still exists in many parts of India. Perhaps one reason for the emergence of socialist parties in India is that they have their local footing in such hostility genes. Similarly, one of the major reasons for earlier-stage conversions to other faiths can also be due to such resentment. Knowing the reasons, Brahmanism superimposed Lord Shiva, Lord Krishna and Vishnu and the more loving and accepted Lord Ayyappa on Lord Buddha with his virtues to fill the void in the minds of the Leftover. Lord Ayyappa's entrusted role to fight against the enemy and his friendly relationship with Vavar belonging to the Muslim faith perhaps reflects the necessity of the time for survival of the school of thought under Brahmanism. The switch over from nonvegetarianism to vegetarianism can also be a great sacrifice to appease the people. When you carry out detailed studies, the installation of various deities in doubted Buddha Viharas, you may perhaps observe certain definite relations for the choice of deities such as Lord Shiva, Lord Vishnu and Krishna, Lord Subrahmanya/Muruga, Lord Ayyappa and Mother Gods such as Bhadrakali based on local preference. I feel that the whole process was designed to meet local needs, to appease the vast majority and to fill the vacuum caused through uprooting a millennium-old culture and a matured civilization. Perhaps this is one of the longest civil wars fought in the history of the world; but it remains less recorded because of the fear created."

Tina intervened,

"Most of the sculptures in the temples of Orissa show lions overpowering elephants. This clearly exposes the extent of hostility between Buddhism and Brahmanism that happened in those days. What were the reasons for such a severe hostility we still wonder?"Tina said.

"Such long-driven changes made us confused and weak. The stories attached to Jaganath Temple at Puri, Car Festival (*Ratholsava*) and the temporary nature of the deities made of wood and remade every year create the plausibility of a series of changes in the process. The age-old unpleasant practices of the *Pandas* (temple dependents) to the devotees also reflect a feeling of intruders who are in a hurry to make quick money. One of the reasons for the timid mindset of our petty kings can be due to the inherent inferior quality in their identification and subsequent coronation. As a result, the majority of them turned out to exhibit poor vision. This led to further weakening and invasion by foreigners. Perhaps, what made AVP different during his time was his ability to see things in a large perspective as taught through the teachings of Lord Buddha. Such incidents in the Indian subcontinent give us hope for cultural rectification,"

The secretary said and looked at Praful.

Ajith's nearness to Achachan indicated that it was time for his lunch at home. It was 1:30 in the afternoon, and we too were hungry. Achachan and Ajith Chettan left for Mangalam in the Maruti. We were left at the mercy of Lazar, who made us feel that driving an Innova is not less than piloting an airbus. But unfortunately, he had only the narrow roads of NH 47.

The secretary took us to an open-air restaurant called Kalpakavady. I had heard about it earlier and was happy that we all got a chance to have lunch there. The sprawling campus delighted all of us. Arjun and Tina, Alex and Lazar felt happy to move around and to see the campus and its water hodies. We had fish curry, fish fry and a traditional Kerala lunch with rice and tapioca. The restaurant was famous for serving *karimeen* (silver black fresh water fish) of Vembanadu *kayal* (lake). We could enjoy their culinary skill.

⁂

At 2:40 in the afternoon, we were at Oachira. The shrine at Oachira was different from the usual Hindu place of worship. It reflected a place for assembly of the public: sit, relax, meditate, listen and discuss, if required. The infrastructure generally seen in a Hindu place of worship is missed at Ochira. People presently call it *Parabhrahmam,* the divine spirit that fills the universe. The sprawling campus was occupied by the large sandy ground and could accommodate a larger gathering of people. The dense and beautiful Kavu and a semi-dried large pond at the fag end of the summer reflected the concept of *Kavu* and *Kulam*. The layout appeared to be an apt specimen reflecting the meeting place of scholars for the benefit of the local people. When scholars and the enlightened visited the place, perhaps the public might have approached them for handholding, clearing their doubts, curing diseases and for spiritual guidance. The absence of large structures might have made the campus less attractive for conquering. As a result, irrespective of the caste, creed and varna system, people made use of the campus for their welfare. We moved around and saw a few people sleeping in the shades of the thick vegetative cover. We all sat below a pipal tree (bodhi vriksha) and tried to recollect the activities of the campus at a different period. A large bull with a glittering cover cloth, decorated with a good number of small brass bells, sea shells and flowers made of different colors of wool, came nearer and stood next to Alex. Stroking its head, Alex asked,

"Sir, what is the significance of these bulls in this holy place?"

"It's believed that if you feed these bulls, you will get the blessings of Parabhrahmam, the Almighty. Perhaps, the system might have been developed deliberately to take care of animals abandoned because of old age or deformities. Among them, bulls were chosen as a representative to inculcate the habit of protecting them," the secretary said.

Arjun fetched a bunch of plantains and he fed them to the bull. Tina also took her share. Both were standing face to face and enjoying the yellow plantain, locally known as *Kathaly*.

"Uncle, will you please explain to us about the Oachira Kali?" I appealed.

"The time had its own influence, even in Oachira. The area used by the learned slowly changed into the local army campus of the local rulers. They fought here. It's said that the last held dogfight was between the chieftaints of Chempakassery and Kayamkulam. The culture dissipated from learning to killing and later, it was celebrated by the winner. Replicas of such celebrations are still going on here once in a year during the first and second of every Midhunam month in the Malayalam calendar. People madly fought and killed each other in this serene land, which was worshipped as the soil with extra vibrations by the enlightened. People who loved merrymaking enjoyed themselves when their own brothers were chopped to death. The Government of Travancore was able to put an end to such killings only in 1856. The great slip in culture persisted. The present leadership could make minor changes to match with the timely requirement," the secretary said.

"Sir, whether AVP had any role play in Oachira during his days of social activism?" Praful asked.

"This place was one of his favorite locations for meeting people and listening to them. It's said that during his visits, he loved to spend a couple of hours in the *Kavu* with a few chosen friends. During such visit, he carried lunch packets and those were shared with the people who were available in the *Kavu*. My great-grandfather used to tell us that AVP once dreamed of developing the present Mangalam Temple into one of the seats for higher learning, empowerment and a partnership building center for the development of the local area. He also used to receive the news from the nearby areas through his trusted friends and local leaders. The first information on the atrocities on agricultural laborers in Kuttanadu was received at this spot, and the first organized agricultural laborers' protest was also culminated at this place under AVP's leadership," the secretary explained.

"That appears quite interesting, because organizing farm workers was perhaps in the nascent stage at that time," Praful said.

The secretary continued,

"As you are aware, Onattukara has a major role in the development of both socialist and communist schools of thinking in Kerala. In fact, AVP was the pioneer in organizing the working class agricultural laborers and in encouraging them to demand renumerative wages. The culture inherited by the land-owning class during the time of AVP also preferred slavery or*ushiyavela*. Landlords and Madampies were not prepared to accept the changes happening in the world around. Even the changes brought by the colonial rulers through the introduction of various laws, policies, judiciary and civil administration did not make any positive impact on *Naduvazhie's* attitude to their subjects. The farm workers in certain pockets of Kuttanadu were subjected to severe harassment by the local landlords. A few agricultural laborers brought the issue to the notice of AVP. He called their elders in Oachira in 1870 during the first week of August. Paddy harvest was due. A large number of the farm laborers struck work in Kuttanadu and in Pathyoor village in Kayamkulam taluk. The workers sat in the shades of the trees near the paddy fields and hesitated to harvest. More than 400 workers registered their protest. They made the usual *Kanji* and *Kootukary* (rice gruel and mixed-vegetable curry) for their lunch. They collectively sang the popular paddy harvesting folk lores. But none moved. Ladies, children and even infants were there with their mothers. The first day went smoothly. During the second day, the landlords felt that the workers will run out of their stock of grain and items required for the *Koottucury*. But they sustained even during the second day. After the fifth day, paddy in the field started wilting. It was a dangerous sign for large-scale loss of its yield. Landlords secretly assessed the status of the food stock with the workers who were on strike. They were shocked to know that they had food stock for a month. Some unknown hands were ensuring the supply. The landlords tried to bring labor from outside. But this was blocked by the striking workers. Landlords sent signals for settlement. Then, AVP was consulted; he guided the senior workmen to insist on current market wage in cash or in terms of paddy on the spot. The settlement was reached. They came to know that AVP was the support behind the striking workers and he could have ensured the supply of food for a few more weeks. This created enmity between the landlords against AVP. The issue was discussed at the power centers. They advised the landlords to be silent for the timebeing and to wait for an opportunity for liquidating him."

"But AVP was friendly with the Travancore ruling family and we also heard that he was honored by the royal family," Alex said.

"Yes, it is true," the secretary endorsed.

He looked at Praful and explained.

"Those awards and honors were to appease the youth posing threat to the misrule. Both Travancore and British Governments knew about the misrule. But by allowing the same, the representatives could enjoy the advantage of levying more than 125 taxes on Avarnas and taking advantages of slavery and *ushyavela*." The secretary paused.

"Sir, will you share the incidents leading to the award?" Alex reminded.

"As you are aware, water transport was commonly used in those days in the absence of the prevailing road transport. There was a great festival going on in Sree Padmanabha Swami Temple at Thiruvananthapuram. For this purpose, from Tharananalloor, the local chief and the priest were taking a precious idol in a boat guarded by escorts. The crew had to cross the river at Kayamkulam, where a few notorious gangsters posed regular threats, especially during the night. Inspite of the extra security arrangement, the valuable idol was stolen. Inspite of an intensive search, Travancore Administration failed to get any clue on the theft even after three months. The king called AVP and sought his help. His men were familiar with the operations of certain gangs in and around Kayamkulam *kayal* (lake). They traced out the idol, and it was safely returned. As a reward, AVP was honored for his skill, courage and confidence."

He paused. His sound was dipped in grief. He perhaps wanted to share a few more things, I thought, and asked,

"Whether AVP was happy to receive such awards?"

"No, he followed a strategy of working together with the government. He also encouraged the loving people in the *thuruth* to abide by all important laws for the welfare of the people, worked hand in hand with the people and allowed them to enjoy their life. He was not a blind believer of any faith. Based on the need of the people, he enabled them to practice the faith they believed in. When the royal family asked for his help, he extended it. But he was always doubtful about their sincerity as well as that of the British Resident. He disliked their attitude to the vast majority of the people and also for their dirty habits of using people for personal gain and oppression."

The secretary had a soldier's body chemistry even after retirement. When he shared the views from his heart, his voice often choked. It appeared that he was unable to tolerate the cruelty of the ruling class even after seven generations.

"Sir, in addition to the incidents you have told us, do you know any other reasons for developing enmity with the local ruling class?" Alex asked.

"I think even his legendary appearance; the inherited richness; the masculine voice; his sportsman spirit and leadership qualities were enough to create personal enmity. At the society level, he had a large number of lovers and a few enemies, especially among the local ruling class and those with inferiority complex."

The secretary smiled and looked at Alex.

"Sir, can I be frank with you?" Alex asked.

"Of course, why not? Sir, told me to share the information based on your requirements. You are researchers and I am duty bound to explain to you the facts known to me," he said and smiled.

"Sir, AVP was a legendary figure during his time. Obviously, he might have been a heart throb of the women, especially the intelligent. Can you please share information on his personal relations?" Alex asked.

The secretary looked around. He looked at me and smiled. Perhaps, he didn"t want to share information on such a subject in my presence, I felt. Quickly withdrawing his eyes from me, he smiled and said,

"All of you are adults. Even the youngest within your group is engaged. So I can reveal to you certain things as I have heard from my elders, especially on an incident that deepened enmity with the ruling class." He paused and again looked at me and said.

"There can be a few even within your group who never like to reveal personal things to even close friends and even to parents."

He smiled. The old soldier in him was naughty and he could read our mind, I felt.

Looking at Arjun he said,

"During AVP's time, lots of agitations were going on. Each day, a social change program was on the move in Onattukara. A few of such agitations were focused on the existing laws on tax, duties, levies, right on property, right to wear what people liked, agitation against restrictions on movements, entry into temples, untouchability, demand for educational facilities and so on. There were a few intelligent girls and ladies even among Savarnas, who were either sympathizing or silently supporting such agitations that the ruling class called *lehalas* (agitations). There was a girl called Rugmini in Thrikkunnapuzha who was like a dynamite ready to explode. But her family, belonging to the Menon community, never allowed her to join. Women were not allowed to take part in social activities leading to social changes. From childhood, Rugmini had developed an unusual attachment with AVP. When AVP was in her village, she took the opportunity to silently see him. Slowly, the relationship might have got its own maturity. She got married to a well-placed youth who later became *Peshkar* (administrator) of the region. It is said that even after marriage and giving birth to four children, Rugmini continued her intellectual and friendly relationship with the then icon of Onattukara. And AVP's resource and power facilitated his free movement in Kayamkulam waters and the Arabian Sea. A couple of his own vessels had all luxury and comforts that enable him to chit-chat for hours in privacy. It was also said that Rugmini had an excellent relationship with AVP's family members; she personally visited Mangalam village and attended important family functions both at the temple and in AVP's home. The whole process created jealousy among some people in both the families. However, it was heard that there was no unpleasant situation created from either family on the subject." He paused.

"Was Rugmini beautiful?" Tina asked.

"It was heard that she was extremely beautiful, intelligent and pious; and the local people loved her,"

The secretary said.

He looked at me with due apology. To make it easy, I asked, "Whether Muthachan had any children with her?"

"You researchers can find the answer."

He bowled the answer to me and giggled.

"The relationship would have been more of an intellectual companionship between two people having similar interests or views on the social affairs that were going on in that period. If we go for a DNA test on Chippy and similar age group of youth in Rugmini's family, perhaps we can further clear our doubts."

He laughed and looked at me. He reminded me of Uthpal Dutt, the legendary Bengali film actor.

It appeared that Tina was the only person who could really understand the relationship between the two legendary figures who lived 180 years ago. She nodded her head in full appreciation of what the the secretary shared. In between, she looked at Arjun and tried to have an on-the-spot assessment of his mind as well.

Praful and the secretary appeared winding up the postlunch chit-chat. Tina, who was sitting on the fine white sand, was reluctant to get up. Perhaps, she wanted more on AVP–Rugmini's story. Arjun helped her get up, and we moved to the temple at Thrikkunnapuzha. It was almost 4:30 in the evening and we hoped our president would be present at the temple gate.

***

We sat with the president in a small restaurant very near the front gate of Sree Dharma Sastha Kshethram at Thrikkunnapuzha. The president was all cheerful, and he introduced our team to his known people in the restaurant. In a small place, there can't be any secret, unlike in Delhi where you can't smile and get away from the familiar faces.

One elder with a Muslim cap and beard came close to Tina and smiled. Tina looked at him and reciprocated with a rationed smile. He asked in Hindi.

"Are you from Orissa?"

Tina nodded, "yes." He looked at Arjun and said,

"I'm sure, you too are from Orissa. I was also in Orissa; I worked in Tata Steel for thirty-two years."

He smiled, quickly collected a few *pazhampori* (fried tropical banana) from the display stand and gave one piece each to us. Except the president, all of us accepted *pazhampori.*

"I am Siraj Muhammed. I belong to this place but lived for three decades in Jamshedpur."

They switched over to Oriya. And, we all noticed the instant comradeship of a common language and smiled. The workers in the restaurant and their clients looked at Siraj with appreciation.

The shop owner came near to the president and whispered while serving us tea.

The president closely observed Siraj and his friendliness to those youth from Orissa where he had lived for a lifetime. He gestured Alex to take a few snaps. With the silent consent of all, he clicked.

"President Sahab, will you please brief us on the importance of this temple?" Praful asked.

"There are many stories on Thrikkunnapuzha Sastha temple. However, the nearness of the temple to the antient site Sree Moolavasam, the Buddhist center submerged under sea, perhaps give clues on the reestablishment of the seat in later years and its conversion to one of the Sastha Temples. A new colony of Savarnas might have emerged around the temple. Perhaps, they themselves were the new converts to Brahmanism from the local people. Slowly, with the support of the local chief, they controlled the locally available resources such as land, labor and capital in the name of God. The center was slowly elevated to the status of one of the four most important places for Shradham, the rituals were performed in memory of the forefathers and an institutionalization process for continuous income generation got well established," he added,

"The importance of similar places at Thiruvallam, Varkala, Thirunelly, Thirumullavaram, Thirunavaya and Thiruvilwamala need careful studies to dwell deep on their historical importance as major cultural seats and the conversion of them for *Shradham*-related ritual purposes. Locations of Sabarimala, the temple at Thrikkunnapuzha and the submerged Sree Moolavasam have certain geographical specifications. Similarly, the thrity-six major Sastha Temples claimed by the Brahmins to have been established by Lord Parasurama contain within them many facts on our hidden realities. To me, conversion of these seats of learning into mere income-generating centers for a group of vested interests and pushing the vast majority into the Dark Age for more than 800 years is one of the larger social crimes committed by us. The realization of these facts is essential for our own rebuilding process. It all happened; we should develop a mature mindset to patiently learn from our past and free ourself from the myth used for enslaving the majority."

"But sir, if one among us has committed a crime, is it not punishable?" Alex asked.

"Yes, it's punishable if it is at the micro level. If such incidents happened at the national level, we can carry out corrections only through reformation. In free India, we should collectively do it for our own rebuilding process. You, researchers, have a major role to unearth the facts and convince the people with the reality and not through myth, as was done by our own brothers," the president cautioned.

"The process itself is large. For this purpose, a collective consensus has to emerge even among researchers. The subject is sensitive. It has deep roots in our faith, practices and even behavior," Praful said.

The secretary smiled at us and reminded us,

"You are here to study the role of AVP in Arattupuzha during his lifespan, thirty years, a small slot of time in the 1,000 years of the Dark Age. If AVP could make minor changes, can't we 120 crore Indians collectively address the subject and change ourselves for our own welfare? Each one of us can be within our own faith and internalize those good things taught by our great teachers, and not the black magic imposed by our own brothers with vested interests?"

"Is it possible?" Tina doubted.

"Is it possible for you?"

The president shot the question back at Tina.

"Yes. I'll change. It's possible for me."

Tina raised her voice and looked at Arjun who was already nodding his head in agreement.

The president smiled at their innocence. His eyes sparkled, tears were reflected and those were magnified by his spectacles. On the pretext of cleaning his spectacles, he wiped his tears and added,

"If it's possible for a little girl hailing from Malkangiri, one of the less developed districts in India, why can't the relatively better privileged make the change process?"

Looking at each one of us, he continued,

"In fact, AVP was better privileged. He was handsome, intelligent, charming and had immence wealth. But he stood with his heart and the culture of this great country. Are we still failing to listen to our hearts?"

I was getting jealous of Tina's domination. I said,

"People like Tina have nothing to lose. So a transition for them can be spontaneous. For those having a larger resource base, they will be hesitant to undergo such changes." Chuckling to himself, the president took out his handkerchief and pretended to wipe his face. People at the restaurant giggled and stared at him. But he was in his own larger World Court.

"Yes, my sweet little mole (daughter), that is the problem," he said and continued,

"We all are in our own shells. We feel that we are rich and well placed in our society; when the majority of us are still poor in all respects. Those who are capable of addressing the process of change behave like cowards. Therefore, even the topmost in the hierarchy tends to be corrupt. That is what actually happened during the Dark Period. It still continues and needs to change."

All laughed and I felt they all looked at me, including those in the restaurant. Tina was the only person silent. The president added,

"All of you might have read the news on the ongoing treasure hunt in Sri Padmanabha Swami Temple at Thiruvananthapuram. It all started on 29 June 2011. It is valued at a few billion U.S. dollars. Tell me how Travancore Kingdom established after 1750 AD could amass such fabulous wealth within the past 200 years, that too from a small and scattered area like Travancore where the population itself was less than a million and that too after giving a large sum of money to the British and for filling the pot bellies of the Brahmins?"

We all were stunned to listen to him. Alex was standing with his mouth wide open and he started biting his pen. On the leftover *pazhampori,* a few houseflies spread their wings and enjoyed themselves. The people in the restaurant took care to close their wide mouths.

Arjun asked, "From where did they acquire such fabulous wealth?"

"Perhaps given by the colonial rulers or picked up from the ground by the priestly class or donated by some angels?" the president prompted us to think.

Smiling at the people sitting around him, he looked at the owner of the restaurant and said,

"Common, now you tell me from where we could amass such large wealth and why are we keeping similar wealth in temples that are much larger than our Padmanabha Swamy temple?"the president said.

Alex faced the audience and in his typical Malayalam, a mixture of Malayalam with more Tamil and English words, he said,

"The wealth definitely was generated by the working class through their hard work over a long period. Wealth might have also generated through trading. Under Thrippadidanam (the concept of state being owned by the god), the various rulers and their administration kept the wealth for certain purposes. Therefore, it belongs to the state. Each item in the treasure may have a heritage value and therefore, the nation should preserve them and faithfully hand them over to the upcoming generation. This process will help us to learn from our mistakes. The savings initiated by our great teachers enable all of us at least to feel better empowered. But we should also realize the fact that we failed to invest them during the last millennium in productive sectors and value add to meet the emerging larger requirements. It remained as a hoarding with vested interests and even buried from the public eye. Though it is a crime under the existing law, it emerged as a macro-level joke through the media. The earlier management of the temple by *ettarayogam* (a syndicate of eight and half) is a subject worthy for research. If the treasure has a large heritage value, definitely it will throw light on our larger culture, which is worth probing."

He paused and looked at the president.

"Yes, my dear son, our loving farmers, fishermen, traders, craftsmen, handloom weavers, teachers, other skilled, semi-skilled and unskilled laborers and so forth might have generated the wealth. If we look around the clusters of Chaliers (weavers), fishermen and the Nadar community in South Travancore, they will reflect the settlement colonies for generating wealth. Cleverly, king Marthandavarma practiced methods to keep away Nambuthiry Brahmins by offering *Thripathidanam* in favor of Lord Padmanabha. He imported much obedient and submissive Brahmins from nearby states to assist him in administration. He could ward off the local Nambuthiry Brahmins from interfering in the activities of the state. For manual labor also, he developed the supply chain from Tamil Nadu, especially from its dry districts of Ramanathapuram, Sivaganga, Sivakasi and Thirunelveli. If we study the spread of the people in Thiruvananthapuram district, we can understand these salient feautures," the president paused.

Alex broke the silence.

"What happened to the local people?" He was curious.

"You have to find out. It was not the time for labor migration. Slavery was prevalent. Why the ruling class had to import people from neighboring states to the capital of Travancore? Why there was a sudden fall in the supply side? Scholars on social history have the moral responsibility to trace out what exactly happened to their forefathers in the recent past in and around Thiruvananthapuram district? I am afraid, even Nambuthiries faced problems. Otherwise, why their population fell suddenly?"

Praful intervened.

"Sir, can it be due to their restricted marriage?"

"If the fall was due to the restriction imposed on marriage (only eldest son in a family was allowed to marry a Bhramin girl. Others had to be satisfied with *Sambadham*, courtesanship with Sudra girls. This led to a large number of elopements of the Brahmin girls with well-to-do youth of the Leftover, the then outcaste), what caused the reduction of Avarnas, especially the Sudras in Thiruvanathapuram, the newly established capital? Whether a large number of them were forced to migrate or took shelter under other faiths? Why the regular need to import people from other areas such as Tamil Nadu, Karnataka and even Andhra Pradesh? I feel that with the newly imported submissive slaves, the rulers could make social life more nontransparent and consolidate their power. They captured the earlier Anandan Kadu from the then ettara-yogam and renovated the shrine to meet their timely vested interests. Further, the innovative concept such as tripadi-danam might have been carefully introduced and institutionalized with the help of the imported Savarnas and soil slaves to keep the secret. Anandan Kadu, where the people sat and learned lessons on personal, social and spiritual welfare, was reshaped to suit the new generation, who grabbed the long-time savings of the hard-earned working class and the gurus safely handed over to the incoming generations to meet unforeseen emergencies and for careful deployment of the resources for development. For family ownership and for keeping the local people away, the new rulers built the fort and arranged for a new set of imported families; mostly people from ouside the state (non-Malayalees) were implanted within the fort. Their children are still there, and they predominate. Time has further changed the very appearance of the fort. Now, retail shops, eateries, service centers and so forth make the fort area busy, and the newly added commandos of the Indian Army guard the hidden public money at public cost. The working class who created the wealth was dead and gone. Their children struggle to survive with zero resource bases. They are the Leftover. You may find a sizable number of them in search of jobs throughout the world. Economic pressure force them to leave their beloved families and their beautiful *God's Own Country*. The minority who manipulated the process were once even hesitant to go out of their village. And religious taboos were institutionalized to discourage their youth from going abroad, even for higher studies. Unfortunately, they were ignorant to realize the evils of their own manipulations. The better empowered, over time, used the same tools against its own designers. And slowly, they eliminated them."

The president added,

"If you are interested in knowing the truth, find them. All of you are today better equipped to carry out in-depth research studies and you have the freedom for it. Earlier, people never tried, for want of their heads. But hats off to the Travancore Royal Family: They could ward off the British Resident and imported Divans of the stature of Sir C. P. Ramaswamy Iyer."

The president smiled. Siraj stood nearer to him and offered a plantain, locally known as *rasakathaly*. He said,

"President Sahab, I had to leave my home for my livelihood. May be millions of youth from Kerala had to migrate to far-off places leaving our homes and our beautiful land. Though I got an opportunity to work in Tata Steel for more than three decades, my family and I continue to be poor in this rich land. Even wrong stories are tagged with our family in connection with the killing of our own most loved ones." He stopped.

People in the restaurant became more sensitive. The president stood, held him close to his body and said in a very low voice,

"Who tells you that AVP was killed by your great-grand uncle? Kittan can never do it and he can't even dream of it. We all know that for convenience his name was dragged into it and he was also killed at some unknown place. A few say it happened in Singapore. What you heard are just lies and never believe in them. The new school of researchers will unearth the truth."

He smiled and held out the plantain that Siraj had given to him and said,

"It is too small and I would love to have a few more."

Everyone laughed. The restaurant owner brought a bunch of *rasakathaly* and *parippuvada*. Tina took one hot *parippuvada* and broke it into two pieces: She kept one in Siraj's mouth and the other, she ate with Arjun. Siraj was unable to control himself. He sat in a corner of the bench and sobbed.

Alex was emotionally upset. He said,

"Sir, why such innocent yet worthy people are driven away from God's own country to far away places in search of odd jobs? See his plight?"

The question could once again upset the mind of those assembled there. The president said,

"We have a great curse of people like Siraj who were forced to get out from Kerala in search of petty jobs. There are a few million of them currently in Gulf countries alone. While they sweat, a few of us are enjoying perfume and the remittance of their hard labor. When they return, many have lost their youth; a few of them have even lost their loved ones. The large curses of them daunt us and make us corrupt, immoral, alcoholic, fraudulent and timid. As the smart among us were forced to leave, the weak take charge. They try to project as champions and one can observe their inbuilt complex and incapability in all walks of life, including the top most position in the state."

"Sir, you mean, one of the reasons for the poor performance in Kerala is due to the forced migration?" Praful asked.

The president once again burst into laughter and others also joined.

"Just now Siraj told us that there was nothing at his home. When the smartest is away from home, how can his home develop? If AVP was at Singapore, for those productive 30 years, what would have been the fate of the people in the *thuruth*? It is the smart among us who create value, wealth and protect the rest. If there are people with vested interests, they will squeeze the people and our hidden treasury will swell. When the gods became richer, the Sirajs of Onattukara, where once the Great Mahabali ruled, became poor. Even after three decades of hard toil outside Kerala, Siraj failed to save even the minimum wealth for the rest of his life. Like Siraj, a large majority of the migrant labor returned to join their families, to see them in poverty and degradation in terms of family and social status. Their curse is the root cause for Kerala's misery. Yet, we are taught to believe that the curse is due to the curse of Brahmins. And many of the Leftover still continue to fill their *vanchi* (money collection box) kept in their temples through centuries of implanted fear and to seek *moksha*. Unfortunately, the Leftover, the majority in the Indian subcontinent, fails to realize the reality. The smarter are thrown out each second and the timid rule even at home, in the villages and in the state." The president smiled.

Alex supplemented,

"When the timid rule, it leads to sycophancy, jealousy, corruption and petty fights. It is an art of the timid to humiliate and displace the intelligent. It is the continuation of the unfortunate culture that had brewed in India during the Dark Age. We are still in it. Earlier, it was practiced by Brahmins and then, by the *Kutty* Rajas. Instead of pushing them out, the *Kutty* Rajas killed their own subjects and brought the poor from neighboring places, stamped them under different castes/ categories of slaves, used them and left them poor. Even today, we practice the use and throw culture. In Gulf countries, we toiled building someone else's economy.At the same time; we missed our builders in our villages. When they returned, the economy remained stagnant, but with imported perfumes, cigarettes, audio–video sets, threat of HIV, chocking air and heaps of waste."

"Can't we invest the treasure as a corpus by successful global entrepreneurs within our country and share its interest or dividend as an old age pension to the deserving poor in the state? If the returns are distributed through the post office, it will reach the targeted with minimum pilfirage. It was their forefathers who had generated the wealth and therefore, they have the right to get a divine gift from Lord Padmanabha!" I said.

"The idea is novel. But to translate the same, we need another set of AVPs. Now many formulas will arise for its management. As the AVPs of this land are away, the timid will succeed in its misuse," Praful exclaimed.

Tina looked confused. Alex noticed the same and nodded,

"Where are you lost? We have to go to the temple."

"No, I was imagining the wealth at Madurai, Thanjavoor, Thirumala, Puri Jaganth and hundreds of our larger temples. It belongs to the people who had really worked and created surplus. Sir, is there any law in the land that allows us to have a search for the hidden wealth?" Turning to the president, she asked,

"It is possible, and people will do it. Even the present disclosure at Ananthapuri happened through the directives of the Supreme Court, when the Court's intervention was drawn by a former Savarna Civil Servant, a Brahmin. So, suitable legislation is also possible. But, how we are going to address the subject? Only time will tell."

"Why a Brahmin approached the court is shocking!" Praful wondered.

"It is also a large subject worth probing. He might have lost perhaps his forefathers, who are much valuable than the hidden treasure; or to reveal proof of a much bitter truth deliberately hidden for centuries."

The president stood up and said,

"It is time to go to the temple. You can join *deeparadhana*. I'll wait for you at the temple gate at 7:00 in the evening," said the president as he walked towards the peepal tree with Siraj and others. Tina looked tired and she asked, "How far is our home from here?"

"Just ten minutes drive. After *deeparadhana,* we can go home," I assured her.

She felt relieved. We all stood before the temple waiting to have the *darshan* of Sree Dharma Sastha.

With the divine sound of the conch, temple bells, *chendamelam* (music of drums) and hundreds of lit oil lamps, the door opened. The sanctum santorium radiated divine feelings to the minds of the devotees. The surrounding air was filled with the aura that is unique to the temples of Kerala. The cultural turmoil was subdued in the stealing smiles of Lord Ayyappa.

# 6

## *Heritage at Mangalam House*

Reaching home, Tina rushed towards the kitchen and gave the *prasadam* (temple offerings) to Achamma and Mani Akka. Both of them stood before her and allowed her to smear the sandalwood paste on their foreheads. I also joined them and together we searched for Achachan. Adjoining the drawing room, there was a small room called office room. Achachan's whisper was heard. Hectic discussions were going on with a few outsiders. We withdrew to our room.

After a bath, I felt like lying on my bed and loved to be with my cub. Why Delhi University students call him a terrorist? I don't know. To me, he is a cute little Baniya brat. I really love him. But that idiot doesn't realize it.

My cell phone beeped, and my pulse rate further increased. But it was that Pondichery *kanthari* (hot chilly). How the lovely Bala Kochachan and the sweet Kochamma can have such a whiz! She will be here tomorrow morning. Why such a hurry to Mangalam? I thought. Something is brewing here. Bala uncle and family, Praful's family and this bloody nut will reach tomorrow. She is a product of Delhi Public School, and cracked AIMEE (All India Medical Entrance Examination) in the very first attempt. I also tried but gave up and joined BA.Economics. Many mistake us to be twins; howerer, she is westernized and I look like a poor village girl. How she always stole the show was beyond my imagination. Tina watched me and quizzed,

"Any problem?"

"Nothing. My cousin Suni is reaching tomorrow," I said.

"Oh! Sunitha Balan, the beautiful and intelligent daughter of Prof Bala," she exclaimed.

I felt like hitting her on her nose. What is great about Suni?

There was a commotion going on in the drawing room. We could hear Alex. He was screaming; and I doubted even Praful in his company. We both rushed towards the drawing room. We saw that poor Arjun was being beaten by Alex and everyone around was beaming and smirking. Achamma and Mani Akka were with their kitchen tools. We were stunned and stared at the group. Achachan called Tina, and she ran towards him. He held her close and kissed her forehead.

Alex turned towards us and shouted, lifting up a computer printout.

"Saala cleared ISS and has sixth rank in the All India merit list!"

Boys express their love in a wild and savage manner, I felt. How my terrorist will express his love? He was very sweet to me that day. I remembered and pretended that I was well within the group enjoying Arjun's and Tina's success in clearing the Indian Statistical Service Examination. I congratulated both of them.

Alex and Praful were still hassling him. Some way to treat a young achiever, I thought.

Tina sobbed, and Achachan held her tight. Achamma and Mani Akka reached nearer to her and kissed on her forehead and cheeks. Both of them were in tears. Alex was still on poor Arjun. Praful tried to rescue him.

"Listen," Achachan called for attention.

"Tomorrow, Lazar and not Ajith will take you to Thiruvalla. He will go to Nedumbassery airport to pick up Bala's and Praful's family."

It was a blessing in disguise for both Arjun and Alex. Achachan, of late, is relying more on Lazar. He is a nut. With a bottle of beer, he will try to even drive in Kuttanadu wetland, where paddy is cultivated below the sea level.

Tina took the opportunity and tried to cajole Achachan.

"Can I join them?"

"No, girls need not go to Thiruvalla," he said and smiled at her.

I felt happy. Achachan is like AVP only. He knows where to say "no."

We all moved to the dining hall and enjoyed our dinner, probing details of Arjun's written exam and the viva. I felt unhappy and a bit jealous of Tina.

❋❋❋

Someone quivered in my sleep. I woke up to see Suni posing to beat me with a pillow. She looked beautiful even after a long journey.She was tall, slim and wheatish and her lush hair was trimmed up to her shoulders. The sky blue t-shirt and deep blue jeans looked more suitable for a student of technology than for a student of medicine.

"Hi Chippz (she called me that), I had an interruption on our veranda. A monkey man tittered as to why I am in jeans at home. He mistook me for you! I fired him to brush his eyes and ran towards your room." Suni quipped and lay flat on my bed. She was in deep thought.

"Chip, the voice of the monkey man. This is the guy who often talks to me over phone in an unknown language."

She was furious and hit the pillow that Tina was supposed to use.

"When did you reach Mangalam?" I enquired.

"Just ten minutes earlier. I reached Nangiyarkulangara and Ajith Chettan picked me up. Tell me who is that monkey, a monkey wearing glasses?"

"Oh! It's Alex. A poor boy from Sri Lanka."

I said and looked at Tina, who curled in a corner of the bed leaving the rest to humanity.

"She is Tina, I suppose," she shouted and jumped to Tina's bed.

"How can you be so fresh after travelling such a long distance?"

"It's simple. When the Volvo started, I requested the bus boy to wake me up at Nangiyarkulangara and gave him Rs. 50 as a tip. When the bus reached our point, he woke me up, took out the bag and made me comfortable in Achachan's Innova. And, I am here with you. I didn't want to disturb the grand oldies. Let them enjoy. But, you damsel, I couldn't imagine that you will get engaged so fast."

She shouted and we were surprised to see Achamma. Suni held her tight and moved around the space available as if she were in a ballroom. Seeing the curled-up Tina, Achamma took Suni to the kitchen and gestured me to join.

I cursed my fate and cursed Neeraj. What was she talking about my engagement? Getting engaged with whom? She may have some one in her mind and wanted to see me off, as I was senior to her by a year. I looked at my cell phone for any missed call. Nothing was there. No one loves me; I cursed myself and entered the toilet. Someone banged at the door and I turned off the shower and listened.

"Can you hear me?" Suni shouted,

"Your friend, that Sri Lankan monkey has teased me once again!"

"What did he say? He is not like your Delhi orPondichery brats. He is very sensible and belongs to one of the most respected families in Sri Lanka," I shouted at her.

There was dead silence. I opened the door to have a peep. She was there close to the door and whispered,

"Why are you so angry with me?"Her voice was feeble.

She was different and for the first time I felt she was my younger sister.

"Go on tell me, what did he say?"

She held my hand and was trying to get into the bathroom.

"You promise me that you will never tell anyone."

She begged.

I assured and charged, "Now tell quickly, I'm wet and want to finish my bath."

With a lot of hesitation she said,

"That monkey told me that he loved me from the day he saw me at Delhi."

She spilled out those words like precious pearls bottled up in the bottom of her heart.

I was furious and scolded,

"Look, you just came and Alex says he loves you for the past three years. I can't believe it!"

I came out of the bathroom and she pushed me in and closed the door.

"He tells me that he was in touch with me through Pappa and Mamma and to meet me only he reached Mangalam," Sunitha quaked.

"Are you telling me the truth?"

I held her closely. She was shivering and put her weight on my wet body. Lifting her face, I explored.

"Do you like him?"

"But you said that he is nice and not like Delhi brats." She was unusually shy.

"Look whether you like him, only you should assess," I counseled.

"He invited me to join him in visiting his mom's ancestral home at Thiruvalla. He hinted at me seeking your help to get the permission from Achachan," Sunitha pleaded.

I was furious. I pushed her out from the bathroom and closed the door. Reaching the shower, I kicked the wall. Within seconds, this boy has proposed and the news reached headquarters. That is efficiency. And, my fellow is timid. He is a *Baniya* (trader)! The very thought of arithmetic made me sit and weep, adding to the shower.

There was no one in my room. Even Tina was missing. I dressed myself in an ordinary *mundu and neriyath*, the traditional dress used by Kerala women, and searched for Achamma. In the kitchen also there was no one. In the veranda leading towards the pooja room, I could locate a group buzzing. All women were there with the queen bee. That idiot might have told the morning episode to all, I thought. She is notorious in flashing news and can't keep a secret even of her own. On my reaching, they became silent.

"How can we read the mind of Bala and his father?" Achamma asked.

Women have inborn skill to address their own issues. Irrespective of the age and generation gap, they assembled and marshalled their brain to trap the male members. Achamma, with her judicial talent, declared her verdict.

"Chippy only can kit out the subject to her Achachan. I know that her Achachan can never say no to her appeal."

Achamma and others looked at me with confidence. I remained less convinced and whispered,

"Let us give them some time to know each other. Then if they are OK, I will talk to Achachan."

The words slipped out and I felt that I should not have said such things in front of Achamma.

"What is there to know?" Tina intervened,

"We all know Alex for the past few years and he also knows about your family. Then what more do you want?"

"Tina, Alex is a Sri Lankan and his parents are world-famous medical professionals. We should first win their hearts and take them into confidence. Only then, there can be a marriage. It's not a kitchen cabinet," I flared up.

"Mole, we know that, and we also don't have skills like you. That's why we entrust the work to you. You talk to Bala and his father. Alex has already promised us that he will talk to his parents."

I was shocked to know the speed at which these ladies worked without the knowledge of any of the male members in Mangalam house. Even Ajith Chettan was yet to know the hot news from Mani Akka who was helping me to fold my *neriyath* properly and whispered.

"Mole, we will send these two girls to Thiruvalla along with Lazar. When girls are there, it will be a check on the boys."

All of them keenly listened to each other and I felt it was a unanimous decision taken by the women in Mangalam house. They need my help to get an approval from Achachan, especially for the two girls joining the boys in their Thiruvalla trip. Achamma came closer to me and mumbled,

"You are my sweetest and the Lekshmi of Mangalam. Therefore, you have to take the responsibility of the house along with your loving husband."

She kissed my forehead and trapped me to translate her judgment into action. Drawing Mani Akka along with her, she went to the kitchen.

Others looked at me, and the timidity in me forced me to smile in agreement. All the four cheered, and Suni held me in her hands and tried to lift me up.

At the dining table, there was an unusual silence. I gestured to Mani Akka and I served Achachan and Praful.

I served two *idlis* and a bowl full of *sambar* and looked at Achachan.

"You are more of a miser than your Achamma. She gives atleast three *idlis*. How can my body get nourishment with these two pygmies?" Holding the idli up in his hand, he doubted.

Mani Akka was fast in serving others and she gave each four *idlis*. The silence is yet to be broken, and I looked for the best opportunity to present the subject.

Alex intervened and pleaded. "Achachan, I have a favor to ask?"

"Except these *idlis*," Achachan said, securing his *idlis*.

Everyone laughed. Tina hiccupped and Mani Akka helped her with water. I looked at Alex. He often gets too fast. I was afraid. Everyone looked at him and he tried to rise from his chair. Achachan with his left hand gestured him to sit and speak. In a half-raised posture, he said.

"I love to have these *idlis* with a legal claim of marrying Suni." It was a stunning submission. Breaking the dead silence, those words increased the blood pressure of all in the dining hall.

Everyone got stunned. Praful's eyes bulged. Suni was sitting next to him and he virtually held her close to his body. She was shivering and kept her hands close to her face, forgetting the chillies in the *sambar* that her fingers held.

Bursting into a suppressed laugh, Achachan repeated his gesture to Alex and he sat and continued,

"If you say yes, my parents will join us on Saturday. They have to book their tickets from Colombo to Thiruvananthapuram."

He was firm and looked at each one of us, including Mani Akka.

Everyone looked at Achachan, who was silent but smiling. The spoon in the *sambar* bowl broke the silence due to Mani Akka's shivering hand and hasty service. She quickly kept the bowl on the serving table and took shelter behind her husband.

Achachan broke the silence.

"Suni is Bala and Vibha's daughter. They will reach today evening. Let us ask her parents."

"I talked to both of them in the morning. They know me and my family for the past three years, and they advised me to take your blessings and proceed."

Alex was so cool like Henry Kissinger, the world-renowned American diplomat. Achachan's left hand gripped Achamma's shoulder. Mani Akka came near to Achachan and with shivering hands kept one more idli on his plate, breaking all conventions. Ajith Chettan, hiding somewhere, stood behind Achachan. It was a sign that he was waiting for Achachan's orders. Suni was sitting close to Praful. She continued to keep her face hidden in her hands. Praful held her close and this guarded her otherwise-visible shiver. I also stood behind Achachan and kept my hands on his left shoulder and gripped him well. Achachan kept his hand on my hand and said,

"So many good things are happening in our family. I think, it's due to the blessings of our great gurus and the noble work done by our forefathers like AVP!" he said.

Looking at Ajith, he continued.

"*Ajimone* (loving son), make the best arrangements for the reception and comfortable stay of Alex's parents. It's God's will that such world-renowned people are blessing this home. All of us, the entire Mangalam village should be here to receive them."

Alex cried aloud. He was unable to control himself. Praful released Suni and she went and stood near Alex. Both Achamma and Achachan embraced them and kissed them on their foreheads and asked them to take their seats.

Alex held Sunitha's hand and stood near Achachan. He broke a piece of *idli* from Achachan's plate and fed him. Sunitha followed the same to Achamma and everyone laughed. Mani Akka was still sobbing. Ajith Chettan patted on her shoulder. I continued to stand behind Achachan with my hands on his shoulders and expressed our collective and heartfelt thanks through my grips, and he reciprocated by pressing my palm often.

Turning again to Ajith Chettan, Achachan said,

"Aji, you need not go to Thiruvalla. Lazar will take all four of them."

Before he could complete, all cheered, including Mani Akka. That surprised Praful and Achachan.

Achachan tried to turn Achamma's head to him and whispered,

"So it's all pre-planned by you. Raising his voice, he caught our attention."

"Listen, I've an important announcement to make."

He paused. All took their seats.

I wondered today was a day of so many confessions and announcements. Everybody had something to rejoice about. I wasn't jealous of anyone anymore, in fact I felt happy for Suni and for Tina. This was perhaps how the gods chose to unveil our stories.

Ajith Chettan and his wife stood near the cupboard and I could see he held his wife's wrist unusually tight. I tried to move to my chair. But Achachan stopped me from moving ahead, he held my palm and his grip was firm. He slowly took a sip of water from his glass and made himself comfortable and said,

"We are eight people here at present. We are together, but each one of us is different and we have to acknowledge the fact and plan our program together. Alex was spontaneous; and, I liked it. Here is a person standing behind me who kept her love a secret for more than a year from her parents and even from her friends. That is also an individual quality. I like it. Tomorrow, her boy will reach Mangalam with his parents and their engagement will be held on Sunday at 10:00 in the morning." He paused.

I was unable to bear my happiness. I kneeled down and kept my head on his lap and wept.

I could feel Achamma's soft stroke on my head.

"Her boy, NeerajNeeraj talked to Babu and Laila, Chippy's parents, a year ago. He came here and stayed at Mangalam. On our request, Neeraj kept the whole thing in his heart till Chippy completed her M Phil. He didn't even contact Chippy over phone. Chippy also kept it in her heart and I got the opportunity to announce the news today. This girl takes extraordinary care of each one of us and the family. I'm proud of her."

I was unable to bear any more and held his feet tight. Through my tears, I expressed my love and feelings to the family. I felt as one of the blessed by the teachings and handholding of our beloved gurus. Achachan tried to get up. Achamma and Mani Akka followed him. I kept my head hung and was unable to look at my friends.

Tina held me tight and there exploded large cheers from all. I looked at Praful and said,

"Thank you, all."

"What for?" Praful exclaimed.

I was silent. Tina shook me up to respond.

Mustering all my strength, I cried,

"For introducing me to Neeraj."

All chuckled.

Ajith Chettan dragged out his wife from the kitchen and Mani Akka also hesitantly joined the throbbing dance group.

It continued till we got ourselves tired.

Praful withdrew and was on his cell phone. He may be making sure of his family's boarding the Cochin Flight. He came near and gave his cell phone to me. I moved to a corner to avoid the hub-bub. It was my own loving cub, the terrorist. I was unable to respond. He kept on saying many things. Mustering courage, I scolded him with all the bad words picked up from JNU. I wanted to express my love and anger all at once. I realized the dead silence in the hall. All were peering at me.

Ajith Chettan was shocked to see me in rattled mood.

I returned the cell to Praful.

"No, we don't want the cell at present. You go to your room and fight."

Praful said and all sneered at him.

I ran to my room, clamped on the pillow, expressed my long-felt love to my terrorist and sobbed.

My Mum and Achamma were arguing about the dress I have to wear when the Delhi group reaches Mangalam. Achamma was for modern dress and mum favored simple Kerala dress, as usual. Finally, Achamma convinced mum that I should wear the Delhi group's familiar dress and then change over to Kerala traditional dress. Her logic also convinced us; and I wore one of the three langhras that Sunitha had brought from Puthuchery on mum's request. It was parrot green, simple and beautiful. I knew that Neeraj loved nature and its vibrant colors.

❀❀❀

I woke up a bit late and Tina was not in the room. From the car porch, Ajith Chettan was giving instructions to the workmen erecting the shamiyana. He is an expert in organizing family functions. My pappa rarely participates in such work. But Bala uncle is just the opposite. He will join the workmen, crack jokes with them and even enjoy working with them. When he is around, all his friends will also join him and together they will make it an event. Both Achachan and Achamma like teamwork. I also love to be with them. But mum will allow me only when Ajith Chettan or his son Vijay is around.

Vijay is at Patiala for the past two years. He couldn't visit his parents during last annual vacation, as he was picked up for a special coaching in cricket. Bala uncle has high hopes in Vijay as a promising cricketer of the Indian team. When dad kept Mani Akka at a distance, Bala uncle never felt the absence of a sister from the day Mani Akka reached Mangalam house in her adolescence. Hearing the sound of mum, I went inside.

After the day's hectic work, Mangalam house was again silent after the sunset. Along with the workers, both my mum and dad also left. Achamma, Mani Akka and I were sitting on the veranda near the kitchen and Mani Akka shared the news she received from her son, Vijay. The boy was head over heels in love with cricket. Bala uncle and his friends directed him to concentrate more on the game than on routine studies and helped him to continue his studies and coaching in the School of Sports at Patiala.

# 7

## *Termination of AVP*

The doorbell rang and I trotted towards the front door. Praful was there and both the secretary and the president of the temple were seen along with another half a dozen men of the same age group. They wanted to meet Achachan.

Wishing all, I requested them to sit and reminded them of Achachan's routine nap.

"No, don't disturb him. We will sit and talk to Praful. We came to see how we can be a part of Sunday's function!" the secretary said and smiled.

I gave company to Praful, and Mani Akka came and wished them.

The secretary introduced his friends to Praful, and they discussed on the election results.

Seeing the headlight of our Maruti, I reached the portico. Lazar waved at me and halted the car on the porch.

Both Tina and Suni were beaming and they looked like a few century-old school mates. Alex and Arjun thanked Lazar and joined Praful and his group.

We three moved to the kitchen and sat on the floor near Achamma.

"Now, all of you take a bath. I have made something special." Achamma declared her ruling.

Tapping her tummy, Sunitha begged.

"For taking a bath also, I need energy. We didn't eat anything on the way. I was hoping to eat something special made by you."

She sat on the floor holding Achamma's leg.

"OK, atleast wash your hands and face and come. I will give you *pathiri and kozhikari*, (a north Kerala delicacy, rolled bread made of rice flour and coconut milk; and chicken curry made with selected Kerala spices)."

Mani Akka stood in front of us, keeping both her hands on her hip and commented,

"All the three are engaged. But like children, they expect to be fed."

Looking around, she threatened.

"Let me call Alex, he will have better scenes for his camera."

We giggled. But the tempting smell of *pathiri and kozhikari* dragged us for a quick grab, then relishing Mani Akka's jokes.

Suni queried, "What about those boys? Can we serve them?"

Before she could complete, Achamma gave her a push on her head and said,

"Mani, just see she is more concerned about her boy than any one of us here!" She sniggered.

Mani Akka kept a few plates and bowls containing *pathiri and kozhikari* and said,

"Now you can serve them; first to the guests and then to your own boys. There is enough; and I was expecting *Baletan*'s (Bala like elder brother) friends as usual."

We took those items and marched to the drawing room. Mani Akka too followed us with water jug and tumblers on a tray.

I felt the absence of Neeraj in the group. On seeing us, the president commented.

"It looks like a ramp walk with Mani's delicacies. When Bala comes, we get the best from his sister."

Mani Akka kept the tray on the table and ran inside. She is still traditional and her way of accepting compliments is by hiding herself in shyness and by serving better *pathiri and kozhikari,* I thought.

Reaching a safer distance, she called me by gesture and whispered.

"Look at the veteran with beard. He is from Kizhakekara (eastern side of the river) and was headmaster of my school. He will know much about our Muthachan's murder. His grandmother was the wife of our Muthachan's faithful oarsman."

She alerted and withdrew to the kitchen.

I informed Praful of an alternate source for collection of reliable information; and, we rejoined the group.

Mani Akka's Pathiri and Kozhikari engaged all of us. Alex and Arjun appeared competing to empty the stock, forgetting dinner.

Praful, with his professional maturity, politely said,

"Sir, it appears that Achachan may take bit more time to join us. We are on a specific mission to study certain aspects of Onattukara during the time of AVP. I am sure our secretary might have briefed you about our study."

Looking at the Masterji, Praful added,

"Sir, can I take the liberty in requesting you to share the incidents related to Arattupuzha Velayutha Panicker's tragic end?"

Masterji looked at the secretary and then at Praful. The secretary encouraged him.

When my Vallyamma (Granny) expired at eighty-seven, I was ten years of age. Her husband was a loyal rower of Panickarachan (AVP). During his usual long trips, he used to take the large-sized boat having four rowers. On that tragic day, Panickarachan was leaving for Kollam (Quilon) and took only a small boat with two of his rowers and his personal assistant. That day, they waited for the second rower for some time and left for Olayil Kadavu at Kollam around at 11:30 in the night. Then, AVP was to meet a government official at Ananthavalleeswaram, near the Kadavu (boat jetty). As usual, after dinner, AVP slept. The boat had facilities and with the attendant's help, he used to have total rest during such travel time.

He paused and looked at us. Praful was scribling on his writing pad. Alex, as usual, held his pen near to his lips and was in his world visualizing the moonlit Ashtramudi Kayal, silent and careful movement of the rower not disturbing his master's sleep and the safe reaching of their destination during early morning.

Masterji continued,

"Though, the monsoon was around, the sky was clear and for a regular rower, the route was quiet clear. The wind was also in favor of the boat and the oarsman. The boat moved on calm water and AVP loved to relax. After an hour or so, the boat crossed a place called Kallikadu and a person with a familiar voice shouted at our boat and exchanged pleasantaries. He was Kittan of Kizhakkekara, a familiar person who worked with AVP for more than two decades. Of late, Kittan embraced Islam and he carried a nickname, *Thoppiyitta* (cap wearing) Kittan. As a resident of Kizhakkekara, he could avoid meeting AVP after embracing the new faith. Kittan sat with the personal attendant of AVP and they were chit-chatting. His tiny canoe was tied to the larger one, and it carried small fishing nets and other essentials for his short-duration fishing. A few fishes swam alongside the boat and they made their presence with mischievous slashing of their tail and a few even dared to jump into the air reflecting their moonlit silver bodies. The water was deep, and the oarsman's steweredship was perfect.

Ashtamudi Kayal (lake) at that juncture took a turn to the rowers' right and its course of flow glittered on moonlight. Both sides of the river were with a thick vegetative cover. When the boat was nearer to the shore, a mixture of the familier chirps of cricket and stray birds beating of wings was audible. The air was almost stagnant, and the breaking noice deepened the depth of the night. Whispers also went feeble. My Valyachan with his oars pushed the canoe to greater speed.

Kitten went near the sleeping AVP and paid respect to his master by bending his body. Then, AVP's assistant smiled and they moved towards the oarsman and sat down on the cross plank. The boat cutting across the deep water moved fast. The oarsman took care of his synchronized movements like a pendulum on an antique wall clock. Careful splashing of the oars, the very low whispers of Kitten and the assistant lulled AVP into deep sleep.

All on a sudden, three larger boats approached and to Valliyachan's surprise, someone hit him hard on his head with a pole and he fell into the water. When he regained consciousness, he was lying on the lap of the assistant and the poor man was yelling for help. Nobody was around and the place looked horrifying. From the assistant, Valyachan learned that AVP was attacked by a group of people and he saw the sinking boat at a distance while rescuing Valiyachan. At midnight, Valiyachan got first aid from the local people and they also helped both of them to reach Mangalam and alerted all concerned. At pitch dark, a fleet of canoes with expert rowers and rescuers reached the spot. After an hour of frantic search, AVP's body was spotted near the bank trapped under the dense growth of screwpine. He was brought home dead before sunrise."

He paused and held the hand of the secretary, who gestured him to continue.

"My grandmother many times narrated the incident to us. I think it is nearer to the truth. My Valiyachan developed health problems due to the hard hit on his head. He never could work as a rowman thereafter. My grandmother was quite bold. She took up her family's copra making activity. With the help of the neighboring women she could further strengthen the business. We still depend on this activity for our livelihood. Valiyachan expired four years after the tragic incident. We have virtually lost our contact with the *thuruth* in the absence of Panikkarachan. It is only through Bala that we'd rewarm our relation with the people in the *thuruth.*"

Alex raised his hand and asked,

"Was anyone punished?"

"No, I heard that Kittan absconded and though police registered a *mahazar* (case report), they were not able to place the required evidence before the court. It is also heard that Kittan was helped to leave Travancore and he spent his later days in Singapore. Perhaps, the interests of the *naduvazhies* were taken care of by the police and the judiciary." Masterji paused.

"Can we reopen the case officially?" Alex asked the president, the advocate.

"Chances are meagre. According to the CRPC 173 (8), new evidence or witness is required to reopen the closed cases. However, with historical interest, probing by professionals will enrich the learning process."

"But why we did such cruelty to a person who took care of the people in his local area?" Alex exclaimed.

"This is a larger subject. You scholars have to probe. Whether it is due to a cultural difference between the brutal killers and the one noble killed? Whether AVP was a threat to the rising power structure? If so, what was the socio cultural difference and why the difference even in a local area likes Onattukara?" The president tried to draw our attention to the larger issue.

Mani Akka, as a part of her duty, came to collect the empty plates and tumblers. As she was leaving the room, she came near to me and said,

"Achachan will join in a few minutes. Achamma is wanting for you and Tina."

It was 7:30 in the evening and mum had already packed my bags and was planning to take us to my home. Lazar was helping her. It was a shock for Tina. She looked at me and through gestures asked what was happening.

"Tomorrow after breakfast we will be back and by the time our guests will be at Mangalam. The engagement is on Sunday morning and by Monday most of them are likely to return. It is better that both of you along and Suni to stay at our home and join the guests at an appropriate time." Mum tried to convince us.

Tina and I met Achachan, took leave of him and wished him goodnight. The group was engaged in serious discussions.

# 8

## Realization among the Leftover

At 10:30 in the morning, we were once again at Mangalam house.

I was shocked to see my brother and Aswin with cricket bats. There were half a dozen boys with them and all were gazing at us.

Aswin dragged me to his side and his mother's scolding followed,

"Aswin, stop playing and wash your hands and face and change your dress."

Aswin was gasping and wanted to say something to me. But his mum drove him away.

My phone beeped. It was from the car. My brother picked it and shouted,

"*Chechy* (elder sister), one *Chicklu.*" He handed over the cell to me.

I wondered from where he was making the call. I moved to a safer distance and listened,

"Hallo Chickllu! You look wonderful!" and paused.

"How do you know?" I asked

"You are at Mangalam; in a traditional dress, wearing a *thulasi* leaf on your hair and you look wonderful!"

I looked around. All of them were watching me. I blushed and wanted to hide myself with the cell phone.

"Hi, can you do those Kuchupudi steps?" he pricked.

I was furious and shouted,

"Look Neeraj, tell me where you are right now?"

"I'm at Mussoorie and I can see you right through the window facing you in Mangalam house."

I looked at the window facing me.

There was someone standing inside the room, I noticed.

I ran towards the window and was thrilled to see Neeraj with his cell phone.

I turned; my brother and Aswin were behind me. All others were watching, standing near to our Maruti.

I looked at my cell phone, quickly handed it over to Aswin and held Neeraj's hands through the window.

Dragging them towards me, I wanted to kiss on them.

"Stupid, why are you here?" I broke the silence.

In chorus, I heard,

"Stupid! Why are you here?" It was led by Achachan.

I was unable to control my shame, anger and the sense of being caught by Achachan. I couldn't help but stamp my feet on the ground. Unknowingly I continued to stamp my feet on the sand and Achachan came and tried to lift me.

"Acha, you are ninety-one. Keep her down." It was pappa's voice.

Achachan held me close to his body and I could hide my face in his broad chest.

He whispered, "*Chippykutty*, you are safer in his hands."

I was unable to leave him. All were around me. I was ashamed to look at anyone.

Achachan took me inside the house and handed over to Achamma and the women moved into one of the bedrooms.

Neeraj was very close to me. He said,

"Look Chippy, this is my dad, mum and elder sister." An extra volt of energy alerted me and I touched their feet and expressed my gratitude, love, respect and admiration to each one of them.

Mangalam house was in festivity. And, I realized my long-cherished dream.

Neeraj's mum took my face in her hands and she kissed me on my forehead. She took out two Khadas (bangles) and pushed each one, holding my hand in austerity.

"Beti, you are the second *Mallu* (malayalee) in our family. Our son-in-law is from Palakkad and both of them work in Bangalore." She held me tight to her body. It reminded me of Bhindra uncle, my local guardian in Kerala Express.

Neeraj was standing too close to me. I wanted to hold his hands. But I was shy in the presence of elders.

All on a sudden, I remembered Achamma, pappa and mum. I looked for them. I clunged to Achamma and she kissed me on my cheeks. Tears blocked my vision. Mum took me to her bosom and gave me the familiar warmth.

My pappa patted me on my shoulders.

The brute Aswin brought a *bindi* and asked Neeraj to fix it on my forehead, by gesture.

He accepted the bindi, kept it safely in his fingers and looked around.

Prof Bala, Kochamma, Praful and his wife along with parents of Neeraj and his sister were around.

He pretended as if the *biindi* had no importance. But Kochamma, being the most cunning among the women group, murmured,

"There is something unknown to us with the hidden *biindi*. Therefore, let it be in the right place."

Moving nearer to Neeraj, she gestured him to put it on my forehead.

Neeraj came close to me. My pulse rate increased. Achamma turned me towards him.

He lifted my chin and kept the *biindi* on my forehead.

Aswin commended,

"In Delhi, Neeraj Bhaiya took away Deedi's *bindi* without our consent. Now he is punished for the same."

He paused and jerked his shoulder and held Achamma's hand and added,

"Caught, brought before our court and the judge gave her verdict."

Mimicking the late Nadikar Thilakam Shivaji Ganesan of the Tamil film, he sniggered, paussed, repeated and trickled tears of divine love by using his thumb and forefinger.

All enjoyed his innocence. A feeling of regaining the lost sparkled on each one, and the group moved to the drawing room.

Lazar and team had changed the drawing room with Attavilakku placed at the prime spot. It radiated the inherited rich culture over generations.

I looked around. More than twenty elders, relatives and neighbors were seated in the cane chairs kept close to the walls of the varanda.

Among the ladies, I could locate Neeraj's mum and sister. Prof Bala, Mrs Praful, Arjun and Tina were in delicious chats. Alex and Ajith Chettan were missing. Both of them had gone to Thiruvananthapuram International Airport to collect Alex's parents. Around six in the evening, they are expected at Mangalam. The long waiting was visible in Suni's face.

Just at the opposite side, Achachan was surrounded by a set of local youth. Among them, a few were my friends.

For me, it was realization of my dream. Achamma took out two gold bangles of Kerala style and gave them to mum. "After Achachan's and Neeraj's father's introduction, you will adorn one each on the right hand of the two ladies," she guided.

Achachan stood up and wished all and introduced Neeraj's parents and sister and announced the purpose of their visit. I wanted to look at Neeraj. Whether he was looking at me? I was unable to guess and my eyes didn't cooperate. With an unusual fear and shyness, my eyes preferred to scan the ground.

Neeraj's father stood; and, wishing all he said,

"I'm Heera Lal Guptha, a chartered accountant practicing in Bulandhshahar in Uttar Pradesh. My wife Neena is from

Dehradun. We've two children. The eldest is Suchithra." Turning towards her, he added, "Her husband hails from Palakkad and both of them work as software professionals in Bangalore. Nearly a year ago, Neeraj informed us about his interest in Chippy, daughter of Prof Bala's elder brother. I met Prof Bala and we entrusted my son-in-law to be in touch with Chippy's family."

Looking at Achachan, he said,

"My son-in-law briefed us about the family and we are here asking for Chippy's hand in marriage to my son, Neeraj."

I was unable to believe it. Around me, my future was being decided. My feet lost their grips and felt like sliding down from a steep hill.

"It is our luck that Neeraj could find his beautiful life partner from Mangalam."

He paused and looked at pappa and mum and said,

"Sir, we are here to request you to kindly give your daughter to our son in marriage. My son loves your daughter. He stood first in the civil service examination. He also completed the induction training last week and got his placement in Delhi."

He called his son to his side and Neeraj wished the group.

Achachan indicated my pappa to respond. He said,

"Similar to the experience shared by Heera Lalji, I too received a message from Prof Bala, my brother from Delhi a year ago, informing us that one of his smart students proposes to marry Chippy."

I looked at Neeraj and he was smiling at me! I wanted to jump like Jackie Chan of an English movie and give him a flying kick with my left foot.

Looking at me, pappa added,

"The first feeling I shared with my wife was whether Chippy was mature enough for marriage. I talked to my father and relatives. It was Prof Bala who insisted on the alliance and shared the family details of Neeraj." He paused. Looking at Neeraj, he added,

"There was no difference of opinion on the boy's merit and Achan (father) insisted on smarter boys for the very survival of the family tradition and culture."

Moving nearer to Neeraj, pappa said,

"You have really helped my daughter to successfully compete her studies in JNU and to reach home, even not letting her know about the progress that had happened here."

He looked at Achachan, Achamma, Mum and Prof Bala uncle.

"If all of you feel Neeraj is good for Chippy, as her father, I'm happy to welcome Neeraj as my son-in-law with love and honor."

Everyone clapped. Mom moved and with respect and love adorned the bangles on Neeraj's mum and sister.

Bala uncle called all of us near to the Attavilakku kept beneath the oil paintings of Jagath Guru and AVP. Neeraj's mum gave the ring to Neeraj and prodded him to put it on my finger. Bala uncle gestured him to wait. The lights of the cameras and cell phone cameras flashed.

Mum gave me the gold ring and the elders directed me to put the ring on Neeraj's ring finger. Smilingly, Neeraj cooperated. The loud claps gave me courage.

Neeraj took my hand and posed for the camera to click before putting the ring onto my finger.

He looked in my eyes. I was nervous and wondered why he needs so much time to put on the ring.

I looked at him. His face was full of naughtiness. It agitated my feet first. It was the beginning of the hidden footwork like Kuchupudi. Immediately, he put on the ring and I took away my hand. It made every one burst into giggles.

My brother, led by Aswin the devil, gave a small paper chit to Neeraj. He opened and immediately kept it in his side pocket of the *kurta* and took care of his *dhoti*.

I wished for his release by the crowd so that he can go to his room and change into his favorite churidar-kurta.

We were amazed by the sound of the *chendamelam* (drummers) near our gate. All of us moved towards the portico. The Mangalam Temple troupe of *chendamelam* moved in rhythmic waves forward and backward and drummed the most popular *melams* (music). In the troupe of twenty, nine were girls. All were in traditional clothes.

The troupe was accompanied by *panchavadyam*, with *combu* (semi-circle shaped pipes), *edakka, thakil, chilanka, maddalam* and other *vadyakhosham,* which further enriched the *chenda melam* through one-to-one challenging participation. The troupe assembled at the gate and arranged themselves in two groups, face to face.

Achachan took Neeraj's parents and sister to the gate and we followed. Mangalam Temple's elephant Neelakandan was brought. It is huge and the mahout Soman will look like a doll over it. But the team is in mutual love and Neelan will do all the dirty tricks based on Soman's instructions. Based on his hints, the elephant put a small *pichipoomala* (garland made of jasmine) on Neeraj's dad, mum and sister. Then it took a garland of Merrigold from Soman and acted as if it was going to put it on Neeraj.

With all respect to the deity and hidden fear on Neelan, Neeraj bowed his neck. But Neelan withheld the garland and returned it to Soman. The crowd chuckled. Neeraj was in doubt. From the crowd, someone shouted, "Neelan needs *dakshina* (tip), to accept you in the *thuruth.*"

The crowd in chorus repeated, "Give *dakshina.*" Neelan shook his head in confirmation and joined the crowd to tease Neeraj, and it mischievously patted Neeraj with its trunk.

Neeraj searched in his pocket. Only the slip given by Aswin came out. Immediately, he took his hand out from his pocket and looked at me for help.

Ajith *Chettan* came running and kept something in Neeraj's hand and withdrew.

Neeraj opened the bill and showed it to Neelan and the crowd. It was a Rs. 500 note, and the crowd cheered. Cunningly,

Neelan's trunk played around Neeraj to pocket the note as his mahout stroked him. Finally, Neeraj handed over the money to Neelan, who gave it to the mahout. Neelan took the garland from him and put it on Neeraj. The crowd again burst into cheers. Raising the trunk and shaking its body, it showed its acceptance.

The music troupe slowed down their movement. It was an indication on their withdrawal. Pappa invited all of them to join for lunch within half an hour.

Moving nearer to Soman, he stroked the elephant and said, "Neelan will get a full bunch of plantains in addition to his usual fodder."

Turning to Ajith he said,

"Please ensure that all temple associates are invited and they join us for lunch. Also, please ensure Neelan's plantains from the nearby shop."

Neeraj appeared too conscious of the paper folded in his pocket. I enquired, "What haunts you in your pocket?"

He took out the wrap and opened it before me. It was a packet of *bindi.*

"That Delhi devil has given this to me as a gift. I was unable to open it before the elders." He looked at me with appealing eyes.

"It's a message to remind you to be decent and no trespassing at Mangalam," I giggled and waited for his comment.

"But, now I have got the consent," Neeraj whispered.

"Only to see, talk and move around like the green signal in a traffic point," I reminded.

He was furious. "It is more than a marriage. My training is over. Your studies are over and I'm placed at Delhi nearer to Prof Bala. Why can't they send you with me to Delhi and arrange the marriage there?"

"Oh! You are too fast. I'm afraid you will never give me time even to breathe!" I provoked and slipped to the ladies' side, respecting the crowd and leaving my agitated cub.

***

Sitting down on the floor was difficult for Neeraj's pappa and Bala uncle. Tables and chairs were arranged for them. It was an elaborate *sadya* (feast) arranged on the courtyard of the *nalukettu*. In the central *anganam* (courtyard), people washed their hands, face and feet in pipe water. Earlier, large *andavu* (brass vessels) served as water containers. In place of the present plastic trays, larger *panavatties* (basket made of palm leaves) were kept to hold the used *vazhaela* (plantain leaf).

Achachan sat along with Neeraj and pappa. He said, "Be here along with Neeraj and help him to know more on Malayalee *sadyavattom* (feast)."

Neeraj gave a space nearer to him and he adjusted the plantain leaf for me. His mum and sister were safe within the safety network of Kochamma. She is said to be the most successful Bahu (daughter-in-law) in the Mangalam family. I tried to explain to Neeraj about the various items served on the plantain leaf. Pointing my finger at the items of Neeraj's leaf, I said, *"upperi, vazhakka varuthathu (banana wafer), inchi (ginger), naranga (lemon), manga (mango), pachadi, kichadi, thuvaran, avial, kootukari, pazham (plantain) and pappadam."*

I looked at Achachan. He smiled accepting my minimum knowledge for survival.

Looking at my leaf, Neeraj said, "Now you mix the ghee with *parippu* and *pappadam*. Use *aviyal*, *thuvaran* and *pachadi* as side dish and wait for *sambar*."

I was shocked to hear the details from Neeraj.

"Mole, Neeraj might have taken a few *sadya* from the Malayalee mess and perhaps from Bala's house also,"

Achachan said.

"Three months ago, I had taken a similar *sadya* from here and Achachan tried to teach and withdrew."

He added, "My first Onam feast was at Bhulandshar when I was six years. My school mate took me to his house on a *Thiruvonam* (Kerala festival) day. I never missed Onam feast till I left Bhulanshar. Maranallor Tire Retrading Company is the largest of its kind in Bhulandshar, and pappa still continues to be their auditor. They celebrate Christmas, Easter and Onam; and, I'm a beneficiary. Moreover, my brother-in-law is from Palakkad. A vegetarian family and I developed a love for vegetarian dishes prepared by them."

Achachan was impressed. His half-open mouth was reflecting the same. Often, he used to comment that his sons are yet to be a match for him.

He took the steel glass in front of him and gulped the water and commented,

"Neeraj, how did you like this silly girl?"

I never expected such an attack from my own blood! I pushed him and kept my forefinger on my lips and pleaded to be silent while eating.

"Achacha, it was because of her lush hair and her own Kuchupudi steps," he said,

"History repeats," Achachan commented; and, I wanted to run away from them. I pretended to fold my leaf and take a seat at the other side!

"What is the problem?" Achamma screamed from the opposite side.

"It's the same problem of lush hair," Achachan shouted.

"Ask her to use only the traditional shampoo. Never touch the bottled one, shown on the television."

Neeraj couldn't control his laugh.

"Your Achamma is a fool," Achachan whispered in my ear and enjoyed his food.

At the age of ninety-one, he is not diabetic, keeps his BP normal and also could relish the feast even with payasam (sweet porridge). Without any help, he folded the plantain leaf and took it to the wash area.

Neeraj looked at me and commented, "A similar gene is seen only in Aswin."

"That's why they love each other and share all secrets, including ours," I said and joined him for washing our hands.

❧❧❧

During sunset, we were at the temple compound. Mangalam Temple is 105 years old and was renovated twice. The present structure, however, holds the original temple and the sanctum-sanctorum of the Siva *prathishta.* Its present *pattambalam* (congregation hall) can accommodate 500 devotees. The sprawling campus accommodates the AVP Memorial Auditorium, the temple administration office and a canteen.

Most of the neighbors, Mangalam family members and friends joined the evening *deeparadhana.* Elderly ladies were wearing the traditional dress, *mundu* and *neriyathu.* The young generation was in a variety of modern clothes. A few of the elderly men were also in *mundu-jubba* and *mundu-shirt.* Based on Achamma's insistence, I wore traditional Kanchipuram *pattu pavada* and half-saree. I kept my hair tied in a traditional *kulippinnal* and decorated with the flowers brought by Ajith Chettan.

Commenting on my dress, Neeraj whispered, "Rajasthani Lahangra suits you more."

The devotees also kept an eye on us, and therefore, I gave only a smile.

Moving with the women group, I joined Tina and my cousins.

Tina was curious about the *chendamelam, deepalankaram* and the offerings the devotees were bringing in small baskets. Mum explained the faith behind the offerings.

It was *deeparadhana* time and all the bells of the temple rang along with Sankunatham and *vadhyakhosham.* The temple door slowly opened and allowed full vision of the beautifully decorated and illuminated sanctorum.

The *poojari* with a large lit lamp moved his hand in a slow and rhythmic manner. He offered flowers and chanted mantras in a low voice.

I closed my eyes and opened them to have a full sight of *deeparadhana.*

Tina hit on my elbow and guided me to *karpoora deepam* brought by a boy with a glowing face. I kept my hand over it and warmed up my face with my hands. It smelled unique of the temple.

People moved out of the temple after offering prayers. Achachan and pappa had discussions with temple administrators.

Poojari came and handed over to Achachan a folded paper and he discussed the content with Neeraj's parents. From their body movements, it revealed mutual acceptance of something important.

Pappa came nearer to Achamma and said,

"The marriage is fixed on 27 September during evening hours in Delhi."

Tina squeezed my wrist and whispered,

"It's all happening quickly. Arjun told me that the Delhi group will leave Mangalam by tomorrow's early morning flight."

I released myself from Tina and went near to Neeraj and said, "Can't you stay at least for a week?"

Pappa looked at me and said,

"He has to report on duty. It's the beginning of his career. With a special request only, he was given permission to leave Delhi and on Monday, he has to report."

⁂

The Innova car stopped near the main entrance gate of the temple. Alex walked towards us, followed by Ajith Chettan. Both of them were talking to Achachan, and we moved to reach the car.

Ajith chettan gestured us to wait. He hurriedly arranged the temple *vadyamelam* and the troupe slowly moved near to the car with a pre-arranged reception. Slowly, a group of girls, each carrying *thalapoly* (an oil lamp lit in half of a coconut and kept in a brass plate with flowers and other offerings) and at the center of which was Suni dressed in a sandalwood-colored handloom saree worn in Sri Lankan style. She carried a small nilavilakku (oil lamp) and her face was radiant with the brightness of the holding lamp. It was Kochamma's skill, I'd guess. Suni looked beautiful. Dr Rajarethnam and his wife Dr Lissy came nearer to Suni and her pulse rate reached the peak.

"We were on the lookout for our daughter; and, we are taking her to Colombo."

Among the boys there was a chaos and Arjun was threatening Alex that he will be forced to tie a *rakhee* (a band sister tie to her loving brother on a festival day) on Suni's hand due to her adoption as daughter by the parents of Alex. Poor Alex was confused and he shouted,

"Mum, I already proposed to her and she will be my wife– your loving daughter-in-law."

"That is when they give her in marriage to you."

Alex's mother commented and added,

"Now you are yet to be placed and how can we ask her hand for you!"

Mum could further confuse her son.

Everyone looked at Alex. Arjun and Tina wanted to help their close friend. But they too were confused. There was pin drop silence and the group looked at Dr Lissy for mercy. She smiled and took out an envelope and said,

"Alex, this is for you. We received it by courier today at Colombo. Our daughter might have brought luck to you."

Alex came and took the envelope from his mum. He was in a confusion to open and read the content.

With Praful's push Arjun snatched the envelope. It was already opened and he hurriedly read the letter and jumped around. In the dim light of the *thalapoly* lamps, Arjun's jumping entertained the girls and the crowed.

Praful caught hold of the letter and went nearer to Neeraj who was standing in the midst of the girls in better light.

Praful handed over the letter to Neeraj and he read it and shouted at the pitch of his voice.

"Alex is offered the post of country Vice President of UNDP in Sri Lanka."

He too felt like jumping and added,

"One of the prestigious placements a young economist can aspire for."

The crowd applauded and Arjun as expected returned the severe blows he received the other day from Alex.

Praful handed over the letter to Suni and gestured her to give to Achachan.

Achachan was unable to read the letter in the dim temple light. Suni read out the contents. The letter moved from hand to hand and poor Alex was struggling to get a glimpse of the same.

Ajith Chettan and his team were busy arranging chairs near the *Chempaka Pala*. The sky was lit with moon and stars. The movement of clouds indicated the nearing monsoon. The mighty Arabian Sea was cool and the wind constantly soothed the temple and its assembly.

Achachan invited the parents of Neeraj and Alex nearer to the *Champaka Pala*. Alex's parents asked for a few minutes to pay reverence to AVP and to offer prayers at the temple. With Suni and her parents, they moved towards the temple. The rest of the crowd assembled near the *Chempaka Pala* and the elders sat on chairs and the others stood around them in a circle.

Pointing towards the company of girls around Mani Akka, Neeraj enquired,

"Why the girls are around your Mani Akka?"

"It is for getting the news about her son, Vijay. They are all his fans. Many offer special prayers and a few are even ready to observe a one-day fast for his selection in the Indian cricket team."

"There can be fans at Patiala too,"

Neeraj cautioned the Punjabi invasion to Mani Akka's house.

But poor Neeraj is yet to know that Vijay was already anchored by a smarter school mate. She is studying at the National Institute of Technology (NIT), Kozhikode. Her father is one of the rich gold merchants in Karunagapally market. Her motivating factor only made Vijay loaded with the killer instinct. She also makes sure that Vijay gets the best training available in the world and money is no problem.

***

Alex's parents joined Achachan and his group. After formal introduction, Achachan briefed the gathering about the purpose behind the visit of the parents of Alex and that made them comfortable.

The poojari (priest) of the temple brought *palpayasam* (milk porridge) of the temple and offered to each one of us.

Achachan requested Dr Rajarathnam and Dr Lissy to speak.

"We are glad to meet all of you and we could spend one of the most beautiful evenings in the divine land of AVP. The world together has a common culture, and it is taught by our great teachers. I learned that AVP reflected the great culture. He empowered the people in the *thuruth* and its neighborhood. He shouldered the responsibility of an ideal king as taught by the great teachers. He could even entice a few youth and even local rulers to be better performers. So he was more than a king. We have to learn his chemistry and internalize the same. A royal king without a crown was the image he left. With our good work, we should coronate him."

He paused and looked at the crowd and added,

"Can I plead with all of you to follow his true spirits and revive our rich culture?"

He paused again and looked at the youth and added,

"Similar realization in each local area will strengthen us. We should unearth the reality. We should pursue research to know our inborn strength. It's worth showcasing before the global village."

Looking at Alex, he said,

"Our son Alex gets an opportunity to be part of the rebuilding process in Sri Lanka. It is an opportunity. If he emulates AVP, we shall be proud of him."

He stood looking at the crowd. There was perfect silence. Then he glanced towards his wife.

Dr Lissy stood up and stretched her hands to Suni.

She ran to her, and the crowd cheered.

A feeling of unusual bliss was felt in each one of us.

Our Great Teacher's hold made us feel the mighty values of

Karuna, Mudita and Maithri.

The president of the temple stood up and by gesture he called me to his side. Releasing my hand from Neeraj, I walked fast and reached him.

He whispered to me to say a few words.

I was taken aback. I looked at Praful. The research team came near to me followed by the youth assembled there. They carried lit candles given by Ajith chetan.

Someone known hand held me with unusual energy. I raised the lighted candle and others followed.

I looked around. I looked at Neeraj, Achachan, all elders, the well-lit sky and the cheering crowd.

With Praful's permission, I thanked Prof Saxena, Prof Bala and all the local hand holders for enabling the researchers to make an attempt at unfolding a leaf of our own rich past. I could witness the change process due to empowerment in me and within the *thuruth*. Closing my eyes, I thanked AVP and our loving Gurus led by Puthanachan (Lord Buddha). They are enabling the Leftover to internalize the inner meanings of Karuna, Muditha and Maithri.

# Glossary

| | |
|---|---|
| Achachan | Grandfather |
| Achamma | Grandmother |
| Achan | Father |
| Adipoli | Excellent |
| Akka | Elder sister |
| Asan | Teacher |
| AVP | Arattupuzha Velayuda Panicker |
| Avarna | The less empowered under the four Varna system |
| Ayurveda | Indian traditional system of medicine |
| Bajan | Spiritual songs |
| Baniya | Trading community |
| Bazaar | Market |
| Bedmash | Mischievous |
| Bhagi | Frightened |
| Bhahu | Daughter-in-law |
| Bindhi | Beauty mark/sticker |
| Chappathi | Rolled bread |
| Chai-pani | Tea-water |
| Chaithyas | Buddhist empowerment centre |
| Chatta | Blouse |
| Chempakapala | A plant with white flowers |
| Chendamelam | Drums-play |
| Chettai | Elder brother |
| Chechi | Elder sister |
| Chiklu | Favorite |
| Dal | Pulse curry |
| Deedi | Elder sister |
| Deepalamkaram | Decorated lamps |

| | |
|---|---|
| Deeparadana | Temple ritual |
| Dhaba | Restaurant |
| Galey-lagao | Embrazing |
| Harichandra | Mythological King famous for telling truth |
| Kadalamma | Mother of ocean |
| Kalari | Place where martial arts are taught |
| Karanavar | Head of *tharavadu* |
| Kathakali | One of the Indian classical dances |
| Kathaprasangam | Story narration with music and acting on a stage |
| Kavu & Kulam | Vegetative cover and pond |
| Khandan | Traditional family |
| Kochamma | Aunt |
| Kochachan | Uncle |
| Kuchuppudi | One of the classical Indian dances |
| Kundirikkam | A mixture of camphor and other smelling items |
| Kuttu-curry | Curry made with mixed vegetables and pulses |
| Kutty Raja | Petty King |
| Marma Vidya | Lessons to hit at vital part |
| Mallus | Malayalee |
| Melkett | Balcony |
| Mole | Daughter |
| Mone | Son |
| Mundu & Kurtha | Traditional dress of Malayalee men |
| Mundu & Neriyath | Traditional dress of Malayalee women |
| Naduvazhi | Local ruler |
| Namasthe | Greeting with folded Palms |
| Onam | Malayalee's post harvest festival |
| Ona-sadya | Feast on Onam day |

| | |
|---|---|
| Pally | Place used for empowerment of the people by Buddhist – presently church/mosque |
| Parabrahmam | Almighty |
| Parippuvada | A snack made up of Pulses, spices & fried in oil |
| Pattambalam | congregation hall |
| Pattupavada | Silk skirt |
| Payasam | Poridge |
| Pazham | Plantain |
| Pazhampori | Fried banana |
| Peshkar | Administrator |
| Prasadam | Temple offering |
| Peykooth | Devil dance |
| Rasakadali | A variety of sweet banana |
| Rowka | Traditional blouse |
| Savarna | The empowered under the four varna system |
| Thalapoli | Girls in traditional dress carrying lighted lamp |
| Thali meals | Meals in a tray |
| Thamasa | Joke |
| Tharavadu | Traditional house/Lineage |
| Thazhikakudam | Dom/vase on top of a temple |
| Thoppy | Cap |
| Thorthu | Towel |
| Thuruth | Small island |
| Sher | Lion |
| Utsavam | Festival |
| Velichappad | Oracle |
| Viharas | Places where Buddhist monks stay and empower the needy |

Arattupuzha Velayudha Panicker